THE
SIZE
OF
THE
TRUTH

THE SIZE OF THE TRUTH

ANDREW SMITH

Simon & Schuster Books for Young Readers
NEW YORK LONDON TORONTO SYDNEY NEW DELHI

SIMON & SCHUSTER BOOKS FOR YOUNG READERS

An imprint of Simon & Schuster Children's Publishing Division

1230 Avenue of the Americas, New York, New York 10020

This book is a work of fiction. Any references to historical events, real people, or real places are used fictitiously. Other names, characters, places, and events are products of the author's imagination, and any resemblance to actual events or places or persons, living or dead, is entirely coincidental.

Text copyright © 2019 by Andrew Smith

Cover illustration copyright © 2019 by John Hendrix

All rights reserved, including the right of reproduction in whole or in part in any form.

SIMON & SCHUSTER BOOKS FOR YOUNG READERS is a trademark of Simon & Schuster, Inc.

For information about special discounts for bulk purchases, please contact Simon & Schuster Special Sales at 1-866-506-1949 or business@simonandschuster.com.

The Simon & Schuster Speakers Bureau can bring authors to your live event. For more information or to book an event, contact the Simon & Schuster Speakers Bureau at 1-866-248-3049 or visit our website at www.simonspeakers.com.

Also available in a Simon & Schuster Books for Young Readers hardcover edition

Book design by Lucy Ruth Cummins

The text for this book was set in Adobe Garamond Pro.

Manufactured in the United States of America

0220 OFF

First Simon & Schuster Books for Young Readers paperback edition March 2020

10 9 8 7 6 5 4 3 2 1

The Library of Congress has cataloged the hardcover edition as follows:

Names: Smith, Andrew (Andrew Anselmo), 1959– author.

Title: The size of the truth / Andrew Smith.

Description: First edition. | New York : Simon & Schuster Books for Young Readers, [2019] | Summary: Eleven-year-old Sam Abernathy, extremely overprotected and a reluctant celebrity since he was trapped in a well at age four, dreams of becoming a chef and starts by entering a local cook-off.

Identifiers: LCCN 2018012122| ISBN 9781534419551 (hardcover) | ISBN 9781534419568 (pbk) | ISBN 9781534419575 (eBook)

Subjects: | CYAC: Celebrities—Fiction. | Family life—Texas—Fiction. | Middle schools—Fiction. | Schools—Fiction. | Cooking—Fiction. | Contests—Fiction. | Texas—Fiction.

Classification: LCC PZ7.S64257 Siz 2019 | DDC [Fic]—dc23

LC record available at https://lccn.loc.gov/2018012122

TO KELLY MILNER HALLS, WHO IS ONE OF
THE BIGGEST REASONS I WRITE ABOUT FRIENDSHIPS

THE
FIRST
DAY
IN
THE
HOLE

BEING ALONE IN THE DARK, IN A HOLE, ON THANKSGIVING DAY, IS NOT MUCH FUN; OR, OH WELL!

This all starts with my first enormous truth, which was a hole.

When I was four years old, on Thanksgiving Day, I fell into a very deep, very small hole.

There were things in that hole. Things besides just me and dirt.

Some people can't remember anything at all from when they were four years old. It seems like most people's memories begin when they're in kindergarten or first grade.

I can remember things that happened to me when I was only two.

For example, I remember the first time I met Karim—just after he and his family moved into the house down the road from ours. That happened when I was two. But for years I could not remember what happened to me when I fell into that hole.

Now I can.

People say I'm smart. It's not my fault, though. I never tried to be smart. To be honest, which is something I always do try to be, I stopped being able to talk after I got out of the hole, so I started school late, when I was seven. It was like being in a race, where every other boy and girl had a two-year head start on me.

At least Karim always stuck with me, until we couldn't stick anymore.

The hole I fell into was an old well.

In Blue Creek, Texas, which is where I live, everyone calls the hole an abandoned well, but that's a strange way to describe a well. Nobody ever lived there and then moved out of it. It wasn't a former pet, like a dog someone leaves out in the desert because they can't take care of it anymore. So it's hard for me to understand how a well can be "abandoned."

What I fell into was a hole that nobody bothered to point out to me was still there and was also still a hole. A very deep one.

That day, Karim and I were running around in the woods behind his house with some older boys from the neighborhood, playing a game called Spud with a soccer ball that had gone flat.

If this older kid named James Jenkins, who nobody liked and everyone was afraid of, hadn't thrown the ball so high before Karim could catch it and yell *Spud!*, I would not have taken that last step (which wasn't a step, to be honest, since planet Earth was not beneath my foot), and I would not have been swallowed up by a hole.

But that's what happened, and I fell.

I felt my left shoe come off.

ANDREW SMITH

Everything went dark.

Somewhere above me, Karim yelled, "Spud!"

And I kept falling.

As scary as falling into an abandoned well might sound when you aren't in the middle of falling into one, I remember feeling far more confused than frightened as I slipped farther and farther down beneath the surface of Texas.

Falling seemed to take forever.

I hit things, and dirt got into my mouth and nose. My jeans twisted around, and my T-shirt got pulled up around my shoulders. Somehow, my feet ended up above me and my head pointed down.

As I fell, I worried about Mom and Dad, and how they were going to be mad at me.

I stopped tumbling.

Everything smelled and tasted like dirt.

And I was upside down, lying like a capital *J*, looking up at my feet and a fist-size patch of blue, which would have been the afternoon sky above the hole I fell through.

I spit mud out of my mouth.

I yelled. "Hey!"

I tried to move, to pull myself up.

"Karim! Hey!"

Then the walls around my shoulders seemed to widen out, and I fell again.

The second trip was shorter than the first, and this time I

hit what must have been the flat bottom of the well. I lay on my side with my arms curled around my head. Little bits of dirt and pebbles sprinkled down on me from the walls above. It sounded like rain. I shut my eyes.

That was when I started being much more scared than confused.

It was also when I started to cry, which made mudslides all over my face. When you're four, it really isn't a big deal if you cry, right? I mean, unlike when you're a boy in middle school, when it becomes a completely different issue with all kinds of costly consequences.

So I'm not embarrassed to say I cried. But let me make it clear: I was four, and I was at the bottom of a very deep hole.

I didn't think I was hurt, but I wasn't really sure, either.

I lay there for so long, just holding my head and trying to think about what had happened to me, and why this hole was here in the first place, but nothing made much sense.

I was completely alone.

It was Thanksgiving Day, and Mom and Dad were going to be so mad at me.

I may have gone to sleep.

ANDREW SMITH

HOW TO PROVE YOU'RE A UNICORN

It starts with digging.

Scritch scritch scritch!

Scritch scritch scritch!

I opened my eyes.

Something else was in there with me.

That's kind of like the paradox of being in a hole: You don't want to be alone, but then when something all-of-a-sudden shows up, you don't want any company, either.

Scritch scritch scritch!

Whatever it was, the thing that was with me in the hole was digging. And I thought, Well, that was fast. Maybe someone has already come to pull me out. Maybe Mom and Dad won't be so mad at me after all.

I felt something brush against my foot—the one without the shoe.

I jerked my leg back and turned over. There was just enough room for me to sit up. I had dirt in my mouth, and when I wiped my hand across my lips, they got dirtier.

Scritch scritch scritch!

"Hello?"

For some reason that still confuses me, I whispered it.

Why would anyone whisper when you're stuck below the surface of Texas inside an abandoned well? It wasn't like I was in a library or something.

"Hello? Are you here to help me?"

More digging by my feet. Then a dark, pointed object emerged through the dirt of the well's wall. It was the snout of an armadillo, and he was burrowing his way into my abandoned well.

The armadillo stopped. His nose was just an inch from my sock. He sniffed.

"Hmm . . . A boy. What do you think you're doing down here?" the armadillo asked.

Not bothering to *think* about why an armadillo was talking to me, I said, "I *think* I fell down a hole and ended up someplace I am not allowed to be."

I wiped at the mud under my nose and looked up at the small bit of sky—so far above me. Maybe I was asleep, I thought. Maybe this was a dream. Maybe I was dead and this was what being dead is like: being stuck inside a very deep hole with a talking armadillo.

And I thought, If I am dead, would an armadillo be something you would expect to find in heaven, or in (excuse me) hell?

I said, "And what are *you* doing down here? I never knew armadillos dug so far down."

The armadillo snorted and corrected me. "Well, that's where you're wrong, kid. Besides, I am *not* an armadillo."

I said, "Oh?"

And the armadillo said, "I'm a unicorn."

I may have only been four years old at the time, but I knew enough to know that I was talking to an armadillo, and that unicorns did not exist.

"No such thing," I argued.

"That's what you say," the armadillo said.

"You're an armadillo."

The armadillo shook his snout. A little dirt fell down from the side of the well.

"Don't make a cave-in," I said.

"Unicorns never do bad things to little kids," the armadillo said.

"But what about armadillos?"

The armadillo sighed. "Look. I can prove to you that I'm really a unicorn."

I pointed out the obvious shortcoming. "But you don't have a horn."

The armadillo scratched the beard on his chin with a dirty front claw.

"It's molting season," he said. "And besides, lots of things that aren't unicorns have horns. Like rhinoceroses and narwhals, for example. The best way to prove you're a unicorn is this: Unicorns poop rainbows. Hang on, I can prove it."

Then the armadillo tucked himself back inside the hole he'd dug. I heard him turning around in there, and I was wondering—but not really wondering—what he was going to do. The reason I wasn't wondering too much was that I thought a rainbow might actually make this deep dark hole a bit more cheerful.

Everyone likes rainbows.

After a few seconds, out poked the armadillo's tail, which looked like a bunch of thread spools strung together on a line. The tip of the tail poked me in the foot.

"Ready for the rainbow?" asked the armadillo, whose head was hidden inside his tunnel.

"I guess," I said.

I was really hoping for a rainbow.

But the armadillo (excuse me) pooped, right on my foot.

It was definitely not a rainbow.

"Hey! Quit that!" I said. I tried to pull my legs up toward my chest, but there was so little room to move around in that hole.

I was stuck in a very deep hole, and I was being pooped on by an armadillo. It was not a good day.

The armadillo laughed and laughed.

"Ha ha ha! It works every time! Humans believe anything they hear! Ha ha!"

Fresh armadillo (excuse me) poop stinks really bad, especially when you're trapped inside an abandoned well with it.

The armadillo's tail (and his [excuse me] butt) disappeared

ANDREW SMITH

back inside the burrow he'd dug, and then out popped his face once again, all smiling and laughing at me.

"Oh man! Oh man, I crack myself up! Ha ha!" chuckled the armadillo. "Rainbows! Ha ha!"

Then he calmed down and took a deep breath and sighed. He said, "Hey. You aren't *crying*, are you?"

I didn't answer him.

Because I *was* crying. It was all too much: being trapped and alone, inside a hole on Thanksgiving Day, and getting pooped on by a nasty armadillo-fake-unicorn-liar who was laughing at me. Besides, I was only four, so crying was okay.

"Aww, now, don't cry," the armadillo said. "You're making mud all over. It was just a joke."

Excuse me, but armadillo poop is not a good joke.

The armadillo crawled out of his hole. He patted my knee with his front leg, which had claws that looked like enormous, dirty, old-person thick toenails. "You're missing a shoe," he said. "And your pants are about backward. Um. You're a mess."

I tried straightening my clothes out. I could barely move, and there wasn't a thing I could do about my missing shoe.

"What's your name, kid? My name's Bartleby."

I didn't care what his name was.

I did not like Bartleby, even if he was suddenly trying to be nice to me.

"That was really mean," I said. "I don't like you."

Bartleby stuck his armadillo lips out in an armadillo pout.

He said, "Oh. I apologize. Really. I'm sorry, kid."

Bartleby took a breath and looked around inside our extremely cramped space. "So. Aren't you going to tell me your name?" he asked.

I said, "Sam Abernathy."

"Nice to meet you, Sam Abernathy!" Bartleby said.

And as soon as Bartleby spoke my name, down the mouth of the well from up above us came something like an echo.

"Sam?"

I looked up.

"Sam? Are you in there?"

It was my best friend, Karim, calling down to me. He must have found my shoe where I'd fallen into the hole, and then figured out that I wasn't invisible, but instead was a victim of gravity combined with a poor choice for water sources.

That happened about seven years ago. I'm eleven now, and in middle school. But I still think about those days I spent at the bottom of the abandoned well.

I think about them every day.

They plugged the hole up eventually.

Everyone in Blue Creek calls it Sam's Well.

Some people still wear the T-shirts from seven years ago that say PRAY FOR SAM.

Every time I see a PRAY FOR SAM T-shirt, I feel like crawling into a hole.

ANDREW SMITH

EIGHTH
GRADE

TOP OF THE MIDDLE SCHOOL FOOD CHAIN

This starts with time travel.

I have an idea for a reality television show.

The show follows an eleven-year-old boy named Sam Abernathy, who's been jumped ahead during the first week of the school year, catapulted directly from sixth into eighth grade.

The show is called *Figure It Out, Kid!*

We are entirely uncertain whether or not the kid makes it out alive.

Except I would never want to be on television, unless if it was maybe on a cooking show.

I like to cook, even if my dad and mom wish I would be more focused on other things.

The thing is, going from elementary school to middle school is like going from riding a bicycle with training wheels one day to flying a passenger jet the next. And nobody tells you anything to prepare you for it, because you're evidently supposed to just figure it out, kid. And when the overnight jump is from sixth to eighth grade, it's like flying a passenger jet blindfolded.

It's not just me they fail to tell certain key pieces of information to; it's everyone. The problem is, all the other kids had a two-year head start on figuring things out for themselves, but I am stuck.

It seems like it was only last June that I was in fifth grade.

Well, it seems like it because last June I actually *was* in fifth grade. And then, during the first week of sixth grade at Dick Dowling Middle School, they brought me in for tests, and then they brought me in for tests again, and again after that, until I found myself in eighth grade, surrounded by giants and talking monsters with acne.

The first thing they didn't tell me about: The paradox of eighth grade is that you really *want* to be in eighth grade, because it is the top of the Middle School Food Chain, but when you *are* in eighth grade, you can't think of anywhere that could possibly be a worse place to be, including the bottom of an abandoned well.

The second thing they didn't tell me about was this: In middle school, you have, like, six different teachers in one day, and some of the teachers are *men*.

I mean, I knew that men were allowed to be teachers, at least according to television shows and stuff, but I had never actually had a grown-up man as a teacher. So when I crash-landed in Mr. Mannweiler's eighth-grade homeroom, it almost felt as though I'd been drafted into the army, or put under arrest, or sent to prison or something—especially because, at Dick Dowling Middle School, all the homeroom classes were boys-only or girls-only.

Mr. Mannweiler had an intimidating name, and his homeroom class smelled like damp socks. Mr. Mannweiler told me on my first day in his class I was the smallest eighth grader he'd ever seen. All the other boys laughed. Some of them made dumb jokes with their goofy man voices and bouncing Adam's apples and pretended they couldn't see me. That would have been fine with me.

One of the boys drew a picture of what I assume was supposed to be me at the bottom of the well. But the drawing looked more like a digestive tract, with me inside a stomach. Another kid wrote "Pray for Sam" on Mr. Mannweiler's whiteboard.

Small towns have big memories.

(Excuse me.)

We are not allowed to say swear words. I say *Excuse me* when I feel like swearing.

So, my first day of eighth grade was horrible. My mom came to school with me, to make sure I'd be okay. She stayed in the lobby of the school's office and waited there for me to check in with her between every class. It was very tiring, walking back and forth all day, carrying a pack of books that weighed a ton, and pretending that everything was perfectly fine when I was actually so nervous, I didn't know what to say besides just saying *Excuse me*. The truth is, moms can't do anything for you if things aren't okay when you're in middle school.

I think middle school is the time in life when you first start to develop the grown-up habit of pretending everything's fine when it really is not.

It seemed to me that everyone thought they knew what was best for Sam—what was the right place for him. But ever since those days I spent alone (or not alone) at the bottom of the "abandoned" well, I felt as though everything was just a little bit off. Now, in eighth grade, I began to feel as though I'd been transported to a strange planet where nothing was right. My best friend was two grades behind me, beginning on Monday I was expected to be in the eighth-grade Boys' PE class (which was completely different from sixth-grade PE class), my parents signed me up for Science Club without asking me if I even wanted to be in the stupid Science Club, and I had to miss the weekend working at my family's miniature golf course because Dad had made plans to take me survival camping alone with him on Saturday morning.

None of this was very Sam, in my opinion.

Nobody knew what would have been Sam, if choices had been left up to me.

But one of the biggest things they didn't tell me about: Being in the same grade as James Jenkins is even scarier than living in the same small town with him.

Maybe deep down I still blamed James Jenkins for throwing the ball so high, and for my falling into that well when I was four years old.

(Excuse me.)

JAMES JENKINS, MURDERER

It starts when you're afraid of things but can't really explain why.

James Jenkins walks like a murderer. He combs his hair like a murderer. James Jenkins chews Goldfish crackers for a really long time, which is something only a murderer would do.

James Jenkins has this weird way of turning his head. He pivots his whole upper body like his neck's in a brace, so he always keeps his chin pointing directly forward like the prow of a ship that is going to murder you.

Who does that?

Nobody does that, except murderers.

And James Jenkins walks slowly. Not the kind of slow that says, *I'm holding up traffic.* It's the kind of slow that says, *I am not going to be out of breath when I catch up to you and murder you.*

Every boy at Dick Dowling Middle School in Blue Creek, Texas, is afraid of James Jenkins—even his friends.

Hayley Garcia, who is the president of the Dick Dowling

Middle School Science Club (which I did not choose to join, but was forced into), told me that James Jenkins only wants someone to show him kindness and love. Kindness and love never saved the life of a fly trapped in a spider's web, though.

There are things I want to point out regarding James Jenkins.

First, I have scary dreams about him.

In one of my dreams, I am upstairs at my great-grandmother's old house in Plano, and I'm alone. It's the middle of the night, and the electricity goes out.

When the electricity goes out and you're alone inside a scary dream involving James Jenkins, you can only hope you will wake up before IT HAPPENS.

Even though it's dark, I can see, because that's how things happen in dreams, especially scary ones. I can see, and I know James Jenkins is there in the house with me. He is staring at me from the corner of the room I'm in, just like a murderer. James Jenkins is staring at me, and he is chewing Goldfish crackers—really slow, chewing and chewing. In the dream, James Jenkins is standing beside the dresser that has my great-grandmother's Grammy Award for Best Gospel Song. It's terrifying. Not the Grammy, or the Goldfish crackers—James Jenkins, that's what's terrifying. And the song, too—that's a little terrifying. I need to run away from James Jenkins, but everything seems like it's stuck in ultraslow motion. But I manage to get out of the room and run (in ultraslow motion) for the stairs.

And James Jenkins, who walks very slowly anyway, follows

after me—ultraslow and not moving his head, chewing and chewing his Goldfish crackers—just like a murderer.

Then the dream turns into a television commercial for one of those electric-chair things that help people go up and down stairs. It's called a Climb So Happy®, which, for whatever reasons, has been installed on my great-grandmother's staircase. So I use it to try to get away from James Jenkins, who walks so slowly, he never gets closer than two stair steps away from me.

It is the slowest, most terrifying chase scene ever, and it's dumb, too, because the nightmare power failure apparently only affected the lights.

Then a voice narrates over the horror of the extremely slow, questionably electrified chase, announcing that if you order a Climb So Happy® by calling their toll-free number in the next fifteen minutes, they will throw in a seat belt and cushion for free.

So I look down and see that I am not wearing a seat belt because SOMEONE obviously did not order this Climb So Happy® in fifteen minutes so they could get the free seat belt, which makes me even more scared, and also uncomfortable, since they didn't get the free cushion, either.

What if I fell off? My mom and dad would get so mad at me.

Great-grandma, too, I mean if she were alive.

That was when I woke up: just before James Jenkins could catch up to me and the slowest electric stair-climbing chair without a seat belt or cushion ever invented in history.

ANDREW SMITH

The second thing about James Jenkins is this: He has dark peach fuzz growing out of his face, and on his body, too, and he was held back last year, so he's fourteen years old, in eighth grade for the second time.

James Jenkins is in eighth grade and he is practically a man.

And I am in eighth grade, and I'm an eleven-year-old tadpole who likes to cook and is deeply terrified of two things: being trapped inside small spaces, and a fourteen-year-old man-boy named James Jenkins.

And James Jenkins is not only in Mr. Mannweiler's homeroom with me, he also has a locker right next to mine in TWO PLACES: in the main hallway outside the library, and in the boys' locker room, for PE.

(Excuse me.)

AVOIDING THE DANCE, AT ALL COSTS

We start with heartbreak and wild mushrooms.

"I'm breaking up with Faye McMahon," Karim said.

Faye McMahon was Karim's second breakup since the start of summer.

Karim always had girlfriends—going all the way back to third grade, which was the first year he and I were actually in the same class together, due to all I'd gone through following the well disaster and not being able to talk, and the whole Pray for Sam campaign.

It was the end of my second day in eighth grade. It was Friday afternoon, and I was at Karim's house, making a snack in his kitchen. The "snack" I was preparing was macaroni and artisanal cheese with a wild-mushroom pesto. I was actually trying to load up on as much food as I could eat before my survival campout trip in the morning with Dad.

There was almost nothing I wouldn't rather do than go survival camping, including falling down an abandoned well, or getting murdered by James Jenkins.

"Why are you breaking up with Faye?" I asked.

Karim shook his head. "They never told me they were going to have a *dance* next week. What if Faye was expecting me to go with her? I never want to go to a dance as long as I live."

"They never tell us anything about anything," I said.

But they *were* having the Back-to-School Dance at Dick Dowling Middle School next week. There were signs for it hanging up all over the school. Mom and Dad had already been asking me about it, already tried to pressure me into going.

They bought me new clothes. New, eighth-grade, going-to-a-school-dance clothes.

"I'll adjust. I'll move on," Karim said. "But I won't dance."

"You're lucky," I said. "Nobody forces you to do anything you don't want to do."

"They make me clean my room," Karim argued.

"Well. Besides that."

"And flush the toilet." And Karim added, "When I think about it, the list goes on and on."

I nodded silently. Mom and Dad made me flush the toilet too.

I guess that makes me a conformist.

I wondered if there was anything I could do that might get me out of going to the Back-to-School Dance, or maybe out of survival camping with Dad.

Karim and I saw each other every day after school, and on the weekends, too. But now that he was in sixth grade and I was suddenly in eighth, there was already a lot of middle school social pressure on me to pretend he didn't exist, to not be seen with him, especially when we were at school. And Karim was two months older than me—and taller, too—but things like that don't make any difference in middle school.

Middle school society is strictly ordered by a caste system, and sixth graders are at the bottom.

They even make sixth graders eat lunch before the older kids at Dick Dowling Middle School do. I imagine that sending sixth graders out into the fields with a bunch of eighth graders would be like marching a few hundred baby ducklings through an alligator ranch at dinnertime.

In fact, my parents made me do pretty much everything I ever did without asking for my input—like moving ahead to eighth grade at Dick Dowling, or working weekends at my family's miniature golf course, joining the Science Club, or going on survival campouts with Dad, for example.

But I got to cook at Karim's house at least twice a week, always before his parents came home from work. Unlike me, Karim didn't have any brothers or sisters. We'd always leave meals for his mom and dad, too, without telling them I was the one who'd prepared them.

Karim's parents were convinced he was a brilliant chef.

I don't think Karim even knew how to make ice.

My parents always discouraged me from wanting to cook. It's not that they were cruel or bad, necessarily. They just kept telling me they wanted bigger things for my future—bigger things for the smallest eighth grader Mr. Mannweiler had ever seen.

Karim spooned a clump of macaroni and cheese with wild-mushroom pesto into his mouth.

"You know what I hate?" Karim said.

"People who talk with food in their mouth?" I guessed.

That made Karim laugh. He almost spit out his mouthful of food.

I tried again: "Faye McMahon?"

Karim shook his head. "No. I don't hate Faye. I am just not going to be forced to go to a dance with her. What I hate is mushrooms, anytime anyone other than you cooks them."

Karim is my best friend, but I know he'd never say things to me just to be nice. He understands me. He and his parents even set up a bathroom in an unused guestroom with an open door and an open window for me if I ever had to use the (excuse me) toilet when I visited. They know how bad my claustrophobia can be at times.

Karim said, "I'd never be able to cook like this. You better not ever move away. If my mom and dad find out I don't know anything about cooking, they'll probably want to adopt a kid who does."

I shrugged. "Well, it's pretty easy. Sometime when your

parents are asleep, you should sneak down to the living room and watch the Cooking Channel."

That's what I did at my house, at least.

Karim took another bite and shook his head. "There's something terribly wrong with *sneaking* to watch a food show."

My parents were against the whole idea of me becoming a cook.

OUR P.O.A. IS S.F.W.F. AND H.

It starts at 2:41 a.m.

(Excuse me.)

"Sam? Survivor Sam, let's wake up! It's time for us to go," Dad said.

Dad sat on the edge of my bed and shook my shoulder. He was a little too happy about waking up on a Saturday morning when it was still basically nighttime: 2:41 a.m. is a time on the clock that is too early to call morning, and you'd probably have to be really grown-up to think of it as late in the evening.

And I'd been having a really great dream about pasta with sea-urchin roe too.

Mom was in the kitchen, fixing a post-abandonment picnic breakfast for Dylan and Evie.

The smell of Mom's cooking made me kind of mad. Dad's rules for our survival campouts prohibited either of us from eating regular food at home on the morning of departure, because we were tough—a team—and we would be able to find plenty of sustenance in nature.

Nature gives you more than you will ever need, Dad explained.

That's because Nature provides you with a lot of stuff you want to run away and hide from, if you ask me. And that's more than anyone needs.

After all the trips we'd taken since last spring (it seemed like hundreds), our routine had become predictably uniform: They'd load my brother and sister into their safety car seats (Dylan was three, and Evie was a very small seven-year-old), and then Mom would drive Dad and me out to some random and remote place (this time it was Tingle-Heacock State Wilderness Area) and leave us for thirty-six hours with little more than the clothes on our backs.

We would be *abandoned*.

Then Mom would come back for us on Sunday evening.

If we were still alive, that is.

And before Mom, Dylan, and Evie drove off with their picnic and left us in the chilly and dark woods of Tingle-Heacock State Wilderness Area, Dad made his predictable joke: "Next time, we're doing this without anything, Sam! Not even *clothes*! We could do it! Just like that television program! Maybe for three whole days!"

Like I said, I'd never want to be on TV, unless it was maybe a cooking show, but even then I would insist on having clothes.

So I pointed out, "This is Texas, Dad. If we don't get shot for running around naked in the woods, we'll get arrested at the very least."

Mom laughed—"Ha ha"—as she rolled up her window and waved good-bye.

I bit my lip, desperately hoping Dad would outgrow his Survival Campout Phase before he carried it too far. Naked is too far by anyone's standard, I would think.

But Dad did make us *abandon* our shoes, socks, and shirts in the car before Mom drove away, so we were barefoot and shirtless, which Dad insisted was good practice. I don't know what we were practicing for. The end of the clothing industry, probably.

This was my Dad: preserver of primitive behaviors and meticulous preparer for all things in the future, which included the rest of my life.

I'd had to endure Dad's Scottish Heritage Phase.

(Excuse me.)

Dad wore the Clan Abernathy tartan kilt for three straight months last year, when I was in fifth grade. He made me wear one too, which was not a good thing for a fifth-grade boy in Blue Creek, Texas, to do. Probably anywhere west of the United Kingdom, for that matter. To top things off, it was the middle of winter, and Dad insisted he and I wear our kilts in the "traditional" manner, which made it extra cold.

The first day I wore my kilt to school, I was called in to the principal's office for violating the dress code. Dad got mad, and the school let me keep wearing our Clan Abernathy tartan kilt, which was a great loss for me but a cultural victory for Dad.

Dad got fired from his job as vice president of the biggest bank in Blue Creek because of the kilt and all. It didn't matter. Our family does very well from Lily Putt's Indoor-Outdoor Miniature Golf Course, and it is also a convenient and proper place for Dad to wear his kilt as much as he wants to.

"Let's head up over that ridge there and see what we can find," Dad said.

It wasn't yet four in the morning, and it was completely dark.

"Maybe we can find a flashlight," I suggested.

"Ha ha, Sam! There's nothing more essential to survival than a sense of humor!" Dad said. "We should insert that into our P.O.A."

P.O.A. means "plan of action." Dad's P.O.A. is S.F.W.F.— Shelter, Fire, Water, Food. And now, I suppose, Humor.

So I said, "S.F.W.F.H. Oh!"

"What's the *O* for?" Dad asked.

"I stepped on a thorn."

"Ha ha!" Dad said. "There's our *H*, Sam!"

I thought of all the non-humorous things that started with *H*. For example, *Hurts*. Being barefoot at three in the morning and stepping on a thorn *hurts*.

(Excuse me.)

I followed the crunch of Dad's footsteps.

Dad carried with him the only things we had besides our pants—a Bowie knife and a magnesium-flint fire starter. That was it: nothing else. And our pants were short too, which made them only slightly more protective than wearing traditional Scottish kilts. It would be nearly two hours before the sky would begin to turn light enough that we'd be able to actually see what Dad might have been hoping to find on the other side of the ridge he was pointing us toward, not that I could see any ridge to begin with.

By the time the sun came up, Dad had found a level clearing in the woods about fifty feet from the bank of Blue Creek, which was low this time of year, but even for a creek was still deep and wide.

I helped Dad with the first letter of our P.O.A.—*S*.

Using his Bowie knife, Dad cut poles from saplings, and we notched together a lean-to against an ash that was about thirty feet tall. When the lean-to was finished, and we were hot and filthy, it was my job to cover the shelter with leaves and branches, and to make a bed inside while Dad prepared a place to make his fire.

It was always like this, except for the barefoot and no-shirts part.

If this sounds at all fun, let me stress how extremely not-fun this is.

We'd done Dad's survival campouts four times this year, and we only got food and water one time—a 75 percent failure rate, if you ask me. It was almost impossible to find something to boil water in, and Dad was terrible at catching food.

One time Dad got so many mosquito bites that he passed out and left me virtually alone—*abandoned*—for the entire final twenty-four hours of our ordeal. Another time we both got (excuse me) diarrhea from drinking unboiled water.

I will never do that again.

In fact, I never wanted to do any of these things, but arguing my case was impossible against Mom and Dad.

It was not fun.

But while we made our shelter that morning, I did notice a mature Mexican plum tree and a patch of spiderwort, so I knew we'd have food, even if Dad would predictably insist on MEAT—a fish or a squirrel, or maybe a wild pig, none of which I was enthusiastic about killing and butchering out here in the dirt, without a kitchen or hand sanitizer, or even the proper seasonings.

On top of everything, Dad knew I wouldn't sleep inside our lean-to. It was too small. Just looking at it made me feel trapped and abandoned. Like all the other times we'd come out, I'd end up sitting out by the fire, alone, all night long.

Survival is so barbaric.

IN WHICH WE ARE TAKEN FOR HOBOS

It starts off on a search mission for things we didn't know were out there.

After the shelter and the fire had been achieved, after the filth and sweat, the bug bites and little pokey stickers in my feet, the scrapes on my bare knees and palms, Dad and I hiked down along the creek to see if there was anything salvageable that might be used as a cooking pot to boil water and to cook food—to help us *survive*.

This was the thing I had to try to block myself from thinking about—the dirt and germs you'd expose yourself to when using someone else's garbage as a cooking utensil.

As I followed Dad through the woods, I composed in my mind a recipe for a light salad of wild Mexican plum and wilted spiderwort, but the thought of preparing it with no seasoning, no balsamic vinegar at the very least, chopping it with Dad's dirty knife, and eating it with our disgusting fingers from the shell of a discarded bicycle helmet or possibly something worse made me dizzy.

On one of our previous survival trips, Dad found a rusty hubcap off a Dodge. Luckily for me, that was one of the trips when we couldn't find any water, or anything to cook in Dad's hubcap.

"See how high the creek came this past spring, Sam?"

Dad held a stick, which he pointed up along the rim of the creek bank above us. The cottonwood saplings there that grew like baleen had trapped nestlike clusters of dried brush, dead branches, and occasional plastic bags and pieces of Styrofoam.

"Eureka!" Dad said. "A beer can!"

My stomach turned.

"Oh my gosh. No, Dad," I said.

Dad, oblivious and very satisfied with himself, scrambled up the bank and fished his stick through the brush.

"Did you know 'Eureka' is the official state motto of California? I bet you did, Sam; you're so smart. I'll bet one day you're going to be an astronaut, a computer designer, or possibly a chemist. Maybe all three! Have you ever thought about possibly getting early admission to MIT?"

I did not want to be an astronaut or a chemist or a computer designer—whatever that was in Dad's mind. And hearing Dad talk about MIT made me think about the oven mitts hanging in our kitchen back home, and how I wished I were there instead of here: filthy, barefoot, itchy, and shirtless, standing in the mud at the edge of Blue Creek, feeling the onset of sunburn on my shoulders and neck, watching my dad fish through weeds for a used beer can with the point of a tree branch.

"No, Dad, I never did think about MIT," I said.

I did think about attending a private high school with a top-notch Culinary Arts program, though.

Dad couldn't hear me.

Dad grunted, down on all fours. Then he reached into the mess of brush and debris before finally extracting the old beer can. The can was faded to yellow on one side. It was the same color as the belly of a fish; it had been sitting in this abandoned spot getting bleached by sunlight for so long. The tab of its pop top stuck up like an aluminum tongue, taunting me and Dad for being out here. Around the opening, the top was caked with dried red mud, and there were a few blackened strands of grass hanging down from it.

"This is absolutely perfect, buddy!" Dad said. "We couldn't get much luckier than this!"

I would have argued that we could have gotten a lot luckier than this, but arguing with Dad or Mom was always pointless.

Dad said we were "livin' the life."

He said that as we sat on rocks beside our home for the night, which was a clearing in the dirt with a bunch of sticks covered with leaves leaning against an ash tree, while we swatted biting flies from our exposed sunburned skin and watched brown water boil in a beer can Dad had cut the top from.

In Science Club last week, Hayley Garcia asked me and Karim

to join her group, to work on an official Dick Dowling Middle School display for our town's Blue Creek Days celebration in which we would experiment with rogue, automatic low-frequency radio broadcasts. These happen all the time, she said, but nobody knows who's behind them or what their purpose is. Hayley Garcia's theory/hypothesis was that these low-frequency broadcasts are actually communications to and from outer-space aliens. She had a diagram of how we would connect a heavy old shortwave radio and an ancient Apple IIe computer. Hayley explained to us that in space, time bends and slows down in places, so it was possible that, using shortwave radios, we might hear from aliens in the past or, equally likely, even some of them from the future.

I didn't know what Hayley Garcia meant by time bending and slowing down until I sat on my rock in the Tingle-Heacock State Wilderness Area and watched our swampy creek water boil in some guy's old used beer can. Time had slowed down. It was barely past noon, but it felt like Dad and I had been stuck out here for months.

And I was getting very hungry.

Later, while Dad stalked around in the shallows of the creek tipping rocks and hunting crayfish, I washed a small harvest of wild plums and spiderwort greens. Dad kept getting pinched, and every time he did he would yell "Dang it!" which was the worst swear word my father ever used in front of me. But he managed to catch a dozen or so crayfish, which he imprisoned inside a salvaged empty Funyuns bag.

I was trapped in a nightmare.

I refused to try making a salad. We ate the plums and spiderwort straight with our dirty fingers. The spiderwort was very stringy and bitter. It probably would have been better if I cooked it, but our lone beer can was too busy boiling alive Dad's crayfish, two at a time. As he cooked them, he pulled the reddened crayfish from the can and laid them out to cool on a piece of tree bark. It was probably our most successful survival meal ever, even if it was rather small, and even if, while we ate with our hands, I did have to avoid looking at the dirt that had caked beneath my fingernails.

Dad sighed contentedly and stretched out his legs.

He said, "Ahh . . . It doesn't get much better than this, Sam."

My dad probably needed to get out of Texas once in a while, I thought.

Something was coming through the woods. Dad and I turned when we heard the sound of boots crunching across the forest floor. Boots make a lot more noise than bare feet do.

And we weren't expecting to see anyone out here; we'd never run into other people on any of our previous survival trips. Maybe it was someone looking for their lost beer can, I thought.

Dad stood up.

And there were two girls—well, young women, to be honest. They wore caps with the longhorn logo on them, and rust-colored University of Texas hooded sweatshirts. And they looked like they knew what they were doing out here, as opposed to starving themselves and suffering from exposure to the elements, because they had hiking boots and backpacks and trekking poles.

"Oh. Hello," one of them said.

She sounded almost apologetic, as though she felt sorry for us.

I'll be honest, after the first glance I wasn't really looking at them. I was so embarrassed for all kinds of reasons: we were dirty and eating dead crayfish out of a used beer can, living in apparent squalor. But the worst thing is that I felt like I was practically naked. I always hated having my shirt off in front of other people. If I weren't so (excuse me) dang claustrophobic, I probably would have crawled into Dad's lean-to and passed out from humiliation.

Dad looked overjoyed, like we were the stars of some humiliating reality show.

"Hello!" he said.

He sounded very cheerful and contented with our situation.

I kept my head down and studied the filth that had crusted on my bare feet.

"Is everything okay?" one of the girls—I think she was the one with the Nike hiking boots—asked. She definitely sounded like she was concerned about us. We probably looked ridiculous, and pathetic on top of that.

"Ha ha!" Dad said. "Everything's great! My son, Sam, and I are just camping out!"

"Is he all right?" the other one—the girl with orange wool socks—said.

"Oh! He's fine! Fine! He's just really shy. He's in eighth grade! Say hi to the nice young women, Sam!"

"Hi." I kept my eyes on my feet.

"Aww . . ." The girl with the Nike boots came right up to me. "Your little boy is sunburned! Would you like some aloe?"

Then she actually touched my naked back. It gave me goose bumps.

I could have died on the spot.

"We were just finishing our dinner!" Dad said. "Sorry there's none left to offer you. It was great! We had crawdads and plums and . . . um . . . grass."

"Oh, you poor little thing." The girl with the orange socks took a few steps in my direction. She was leaning over me—looking at my exposed body!

"We have plenty of food," the other one said. "We can leave you whatever you'd like."

"Oh, that won't be necessary. Really," Dad protested.

"I have a T-shirt and some socks your boy can have," the girl with the orange socks said.

I was mortified.

It seemed to take forever before Dad could finally convince the college girls that we were indeed okay, and that they didn't need to worry about us. But in the end they left two shirts from their school, a pair of socks, a wool beanie, some flip-flops, some aloe vera lotion, and a twenty-dollar bill for Dad.

It was very nice of them.

And before they left, one of them pleaded with Dad to not spend the twenty dollars on drugs or alcohol.

Dad got angry at me when I asked him if it would be okay for me to put on one of the University of Texas shirts.

The rules of survival prohibited such luxuries.

THE
FIRST
DAY
IN
THE
HOLE

THE ARMADILLO OF THANKSGIVING PRESENT

This starts with me following an armadillo named Bartleby into a tunnel.

It seemed like hours since I'd fallen down the hole into the abandoned well. I thought surely there had to be people up above somewhere who were looking for me by now. But I also began to question whether I had actually heard Karim's voice calling down to me, and if anyone at all was aware that I was missing.

In the meantime it was just me and a talking armadillo who was overly pleased with himself for (excuse me) pooping on my foot.

"So the main thing is," Bartleby, who was rarely at a loss for explaining things to me, said, "in times like these, it's important that you maintain a positive outlook. Think about good things."

Bartleby seemed to know about how to deal with such predicaments as what to do when you're a four-year-old boy and you fall into an abandoned well.

"Well, it's Thanksgiving. But I'm not going to have any Thanksgiving dinner. And I want to get out of here," I said.

"I'd say that's a start," Bartleby said. "But it's not really that positive when you think about it, since you're kind of complaining about being trapped and how you can't get out, and that you're not going to have dinner. You should try harder to focus on the good."

I pointed out, "But I *am* trapped. And I *can't* get out. And I'm missing a shoe and Thanksgiving dinner. And Mom and Dad are going to be mad at me. I can't think of anything good right at the moment."

I felt like all that positivity was about to make me start crying again.

"You know what I do when I feel like you do?" Bartleby asked.

"You probably—excuse me—poop on someone's foot and then laugh at them."

"Ha ha! You're clever, Sam Abernathy! I like you!" Bartleby said.

I sighed and wiped at my muddy face.

I wished I could ignore him. I honestly didn't want him to go away and leave me alone, but I also found Bartleby to be totally annoying.

Bartleby tapped my knee. He said, "Come on. If you're missing your dinner, I can get you something to eat."

"I don't trust you," I said.

"Look, I said I was sorry about the poop joke. But you have to admit it was very, very funny. Hilarious, even. And if you're hungry, I can get you something to eat," Bartleby said. "You'd be surprised at all the stuff I can do."

I'd already had enough surprises from Bartleby, I thought. And I wasn't hungry; I was just finding a justifiable reason to complain about my situation.

Bartleby turned around and stuck his head into the tunnel he'd dug, so his (excuse me) butt was sticking out at my face again.

He said, "Follow me, Sam."

"Are you going to get me out of here?" I asked.

Bartleby stopped. For a long time he didn't move or say anything, like he was thinking about something, or maybe getting ready to (excuse me) poop again.

I sat there at the bottom of my well staring at Bartleby's motionless tail.

"We'll talk about getting out later," Bartleby said. "So, are you going to follow me or not?"

I didn't want to be alone, so I followed Bartleby the armadillo into his tunnel.

It was very dark and very dirty, and I couldn't really see much of anything. All I could manage to do was crawl along on my belly and follow the *scritch scritch* sounds of Bartleby's claws and the babble of his never-ending chatter.

"You wouldn't by chance have a pack of cigarettes on you, would you?" Bartleby asked.

"Of course not," I said.

Bartleby stopped, paused for a moment, and sighed. "Yeah. Didn't think so. You look a little soft."

"Armadillos don't smoke cigarettes," I said.

"Oh please, kid. Stop it. There's so much you don't even know," Bartleby said. "For example, you obviously don't know that armadillos are *not* unicorns in molting season, and therefore we do not poop rainbows. Ha ha ha!"

I stopped following Bartleby.

"I should turn around. Maybe they're already looking for me."

"Quit it, kid. Sam, I mean. Quit being a quitter, Sam Abernathy. I'll know when people are here. I'll tell you when we go back. But you have to trust me," Bartleby said.

And although I did not trust Bartleby, I started following him again.

"Where are you taking me?" I asked.

Bartleby said, "Just trust me. Have you ever heard the story of *A Christmas Carol*? Anyhow, it's just a bunch of hoo-haw, but it's about this mean old man who gets visited on Christmas by three ghosts—one from the present, one from the past, and one from the future. And they *change his life*."

I knew the story. Who doesn't?

Bartleby went on, "Well, Sam Abernathy, guess what. I happen to be the Armadillo of Thanksgiving Present."

"Oh," I said.

"Ha ha! Not really! I'm lying again!" Bartleby said. "You really shouldn't be so trusting of strangers, Sam!"

I decided my dislike for Bartleby had blossomed to hatred.

And Bartleby, true to his nature, went on, "But I *am* going to change your life, Sam! After all, I kind of owe it to you, considering what I did back there in your hole."

Bartleby stopped.

"Hmm . . . "

"What is it?" I asked.

"I can't remember which way I came," Bartleby said.

"What do you mean? You came this way. My well is behind us," I said.

"No. The tunnels. There are three of them here. I can't remember which one I came down when I heard you crying."

"We should go back, then," I said. "I don't want to get lost, and someone will be looking for me soon."

Bartleby did not respond to my suggestion that we turn back. He sat there for a while, with his (excuse me) butt blocking our path forward. I heard him whisper to himself "Eenie meenie miney mo."

"What are you doing?" I said.

Bartleby cleared his armadillo throat. "Nah . . . Nothing. I remember now. Come on, follow me."

And when Bartleby crawled forward, I could see the three black mouths of tunnels ahead of us. It was like Bartleby had his own city down here. He probably had to, in order to avoid all the enemies he'd undoubtedly made up above in the world of sunlight, the living, and the sane.

But I couldn't tell where he'd gone.

"Which one did you take?" I asked.

Bartleby's voice came out of the hole in the middle. "This one!"

I crawled inside.

"Do any of these tunnels lead to the *outside*?" I asked.

"Of course!" Bartleby said. "The one *you* came down does! Ha ha!"

After a few minutes of silent belly crawling in the dark, Bartleby said, "Hey, you're not crying, are you?"

My voice cracked, and (excuse me) snot ran from my nose.

"No," I lied.

"Aww, now, toughen up, Sam," Bartleby said.

It sounded like something my dad would say.

I sniffled. There was nowhere and nothing to wipe my nose on. It was so disgusting.

Thump.

"Oops. Hey, I've been looking for this," Bartleby said.

"Looking for what?"

"Well, I'm sorry to say I took the wrong tunnel, Sam. But I finally found Ethan Pixler!"

"Who?"

"Ethan Pixler. Jeez!" Bartleby said. He sounded disgusted that he had to repeat himself, like I was stupid or something.

And Bartleby added, "See if you can squeeze up here next to me. Ethan Pixler's here!"

I crawled through the damp dirt until I was beside Bartleby, preparing to meet this Ethan Pixler guy, whoever that was.

AT LEAST I AM BETTER OFF
THAN ETHAN PIXLER

It starts with a really old coffin.

It seemed Ethan Pixler was quite dead.

I could tell that because there were two dates engraved in a tarnished brass plaque on the long side of the coffin Bartleby had run into.

The plaque said this:

ETHAN EVAN PIXLER

1834–1888

CHOKED ON SOMETHING TOO BIG TO SWALLOW:

A NOOSE

ELECTION DAY 1888

"You tunneled into a graveyard?" I asked. "Why would anyone want to dig a tunnel into a graveyard?"

Bartleby, who didn't have much in the way of shoulders, shrugged. "It's not much of a graveyard. Ethan Pixler's the only dead guy down here that I know of. Well, besides you and me,

I suppose. But it's not often you find a coffin buried fifty-four feet underground."

"We're fifty-four feet down?"

"Give or take a few feet," Bartleby said.

And Bartleby waved his right claw at the coffin, which was about one-third embedded into the side of the chamber Bartleby had apparently excavated around it. He said, "Sam Abernathy, meet Ethan Pixler. Ethan, this is Sam Abernathy. He's new here. And he's . . . How old did you say you are, Sam?"

"Four," I said. "I'm four years old. Does he actually talk to you?"

Bartleby scratched at his beard. "Um . . . yes. Yes, he does, Sam, because Ethan Pixler happens to be the real-life Ghost of Thanksgiving Past."

"He *is*?"

Bartleby slapped his claw against the side of Ethan Pixler's coffin and laughed again. "Ha ha! No, Sam! He's been dead for more than a hundred years. Of course he doesn't talk! I did it again! Man, I crack myself up! Ha ha ha! *The Ghost of Thanksgiving Past!*"

I'd had it with Bartleby. I thought about turning around and leaving him and all his dumb foolish stories and crawling back to my abandoned well, where I could hopefully be left alone. But then the idea struck me that maybe I could get even with Bartleby, and play a trick on him, and make him feel stupid for once.

I said, "Shh! Did you hear that?"

Bartleby's eyes narrowed, which was difficult on account of the fact that an armadillo's eyes are usually non-expressive.

"Hear what?" he whispered.

"I . . . I think he really did say something to us, Bartleby."

I crawled close enough to Ethan Pixler's more-than-one-hundred-year-old coffin to press an ear up to it, which was kind of disgusting.

And I don't know which of us—Bartleby or myself—screamed the loudest when we heard this: "Sam? Sam Abernathy?"

We both screamed really loud.

If there was room enough, I would have jumped out of my pants. As it was, I nearly (excuse me) peed in them, anyway.

But in my defense (and Bartleby's, too, I suppose), nobody ever expects a voice from a more-than-one-hundred-year-old coffin to call out to you. And I found myself thinking that it was not surprising that dead Ethan Evan Pixler's initials spelled "Eep!"

"Sam? If you can, sweetie, can you say something to let us know you're in there, bud?"

But the voice was not coming from dead Ethan Pixler.

It was coming from the well, and it was my dad.

They were looking for me.

EIGHTH GRADE

GROWN-UP BARBARISM

This starts on Monday, in my first eighth-grade Boys' PE class.

(Excuse me.)

This was the only other class of mine that had a *man* for a teacher.

Everything about eighth-grade Boys' PE was all man, man, man. It was unnerving and disgusting, like survival campouts with forty eighth-grade Dads.

In sixth-grade PE, boys and girls played together—games like four square or handball—and we got to keep our clothes on. Nobody ever told me about how when you get into grades seven and eight, you are put in classes only with boys and have *men teachers*, and they make you take off your clothes in front of everyone and change into *uniforms*—and worst of all, they make us strip (excuse me) naked and take (excuse me) showers together when the coach decides we are too sweaty.

Nobody ever—*ever*—told me about that until I showed up for Coach Bovard's eighth-grade Boys' PE class, and by that time it was far too late for anyone to do anything about it.

I had no idea, since the first few days of class all we boys did was sit on bleachers inside the gymnasium and read books. I'd assumed eighth-grade Boys' PE class was about reading, which was fine with me.

Maybe it was my fault for not looking at the eighth-grade Boys' PE class orientation pamphlet Coach Bovard had given me when I was moved ahead two grades. I just figured the pamphlet was about not swearing, or raising your hand when you wanted to say something. But the pamphlet was not about swearing or raising hands at all. It had all these specific policies about the exact kinds of clothes we had to wear in PE and what we were allowed and not allowed to wear under them or over them; how many exact minutes we had to change into those uniforms; how we were not allowed to chew gum or talk at all when we were inside the locker room; how we were required to use only roll-on or solid deodorant (which I've never used in my life) because spray deodorant was dangerous, especially to kids with asthma; and how we were required to bring our own shampoo and towels from home and always bring all our clothes home on Fridays to wash them; and how since nobody likes to sit next to a stinky boy in class, that whenever Coach Bovard turned on the showers it meant we had to take off all our clothes in front of everyone else in Coach Bovard's (excuse me) dumb PE class, and we had to take showers together and then get dressed back into our OUTFITS OF NON-NAKED CIVILIZATION in exactly three minutes so we could get to our next class.

(Excuse me.)

I did not figure any of this out until after I opened the pillowcase-bag Mom had left out for me and saw that it contained a white T-shirt with my last name written in permanent marker across the chest, a pair of yellow Dick Dowling Middle School Mustangs gym shorts (that also had "Abernathy" written across the hem of the right leg), some new white socks, gym shoes, a towel, shampoo, and a stick of deodorant.

I wanted to run away from home, and maybe get a job as a line cook at Waffle House. As far as I know, Waffle House cooks are not required to take showers together.

To make matters worse, on this first Monday in the grown-up barbarism of Coach Bovard's PE class, a day when I was all nicked up and viciously sunburned after Dad's survival campout weekend, I found myself sitting down on a locker room bench and getting undressed for the first time ever in front of a bunch of other boys, and the one eighth grader assigned to the locker right next to mine happened to be James Jenkins, man-boy murderer, who took his clothes off really slowly without moving his head and just silently stared and stared at me, like a murderer.

"Hey, Well Boy," James Jenkins said in his slow monotone, "you're all sunburned."

I nearly tripped and fell down pulling up my shorts. I wanted James Jenkins to stop looking at me in my underwear.

"I went camping with my dad," I explained, tugging my (excuse me) stupid T-shirt with my name on it over my head.

"Oh. Fun." James Jenkins's voice was about as enthusiastic as a funeral director's.

I imagined he thought camping was fun because it offered the likelihood of killing things.

Then Coach Bovard screamed at me and James, who just stood there, unmoving, in his underwear.

"What part of NO TALKING IN THE LOCKER ROOM do you nitwits not understand?" Coach Bovard yelled so loud, it echoed from the concrete walls and porcelain tiles of the locker room.

Every boy in the class stopped breathing and froze in place. I was terrified.

I had never been yelled at by a grown man while I was taking off my clothes in my entire life. I almost started to cry, but there is nothing worse a boy in eighth grade can do than cry in front of a bunch of other eighth-grade boys in their underwear.

James Jenkins, without moving his head, slowly pulled on his gym shorts.

After we all got dressed into our uniforms and learned how to stand on our numbered spots on the outdoor basketball courts so Coach Bovard could take roll and yell at us some more, Coach Bovard made the whole class run two miles on the track.

I'm smaller than everyone else in Boys' PE. Some boys like to make a contest out of everything and try hard to be the fastest in the class. I can never keep up with the pack, probably due to the shortness of my legs. But James Jenkins ran even slower than I did. Like a nightmare, James Jenkins, who never seemed to get out of breath on the two-mile run, stayed about ten feet behind me. When I'd glance back, there he was, staring right at me, not moving his head, just following calmly and slowly.

Halfway around the seventh lap on the track, James Jenkins caught up to me. I thought, this is it, I am going to die, which I decided was probably better than ever going back inside that locker room.

James Jenkins, staring directly ahead and not looking at me, said, "Don't be scared of Blow-vard. He does this every year on the first day of PE class—finds someone to scream at, then makes us run so he can climb up the bleachers and have a cigarette while he watches us."

I figured, out of all of us, James Jenkins would be the most familiar with Coach Bovard's first-day routine, since he'd been held back for an extra trip through eighth grade. And for just a moment I thought James Jenkins, who was responsible for me falling into an abandoned well when I was four and my extreme claustrophobia and not talking for two years, was actually being *kind* to me.

But then James Jenkins said this: "And that's why all these guys are going to hate you for the rest of the year, Well Boy."

And at the end of the period, after we all straggled in from the two-mile run, Coach Bovard informed us that we were disgusting and sweaty, and that we all had to take showers.

I nearly lost consciousness from the fear and humiliation of the day.

THE RINGS OF SATURN

It starts the day of Dick Dowling Middle School's Back-to-
School Dance.

There were threats, admonitions about my future—the kinds of things Mom and Dad always did. I recognize they wanted their version of what was "best" for me. They were so concerned now, *after* I'd skipped ahead two years in a sociological time warp, about my fitting in—or, more precisely, rising to the top of the academic caste. They had already planned out my courses in ninth grade next year at Blue Creek Magnet High School and had decided that I would take an emphasis in physics and engineering. The magnet school was a science and math school. I felt as enthusiastic about a science and math school as I'd felt about drinking boiled creek water from some stranger's used beer can.

Mom and Dad had probably already chosen a spouse for me and put a down payment on a starter home too, for all I knew.

So that day, Mom and Dad *made me* wear the new checkered button-up shirt they bought specifically so they could also force me to go to Dick Dowling Middle School's Back-to-School Dance. They made me tuck my shirt into my brand new pants, which were held up by a brand new shiny leather belt that matched my brand new shiny black loafers. I felt like I'd been imprisoned in the two-dimensional universe of a glossy photograph inside a JCPenney catalog.

What do people actually *do* at dances, anyway?

I had never been to a dance in my life.

And I may have known next to nothing about middle school, having at eleven years of age been skipped directly from week one of sixth grade to week two of eighth grade, but I did know that you just don't show up in a brand new blue-and-pink-checkered shirt that no other boy in Dick Dowling Middle School would ever wear without running the risk of being made fun of for the next nine months, and probably into (excuse me) dumb magnet high school as well.

"Maybe you should punish me by making me stay home," I suggested to Mom, after she asked what she was going to *do* with me. Mom's question was the result of the fact that I had misplaced—or something—my permission slip for the dance. Everyone had to turn in a permission slip. It was like a contract that told parents what exact time they had to come to pick us up, and made us promise not to expose our (excuse me) underwear or dance in ways that were (excuse me) sexually suggestive.

Really. They have to make eighth-grade boys sign contracts about those things.

I didn't get it. It was terrifying to me.

Mom combed my hair. She put gel in it.

I was certain no other eighth-grade boy at Dick Dowling was getting his hair combed by his mom that night.

She said, "I'm sure they'll have extra permission slips at the door."

The dance ended up being like a journey into another version of reality.

First off, if there were any sixth graders there, they made themselves invisible, which meant that as far as I could tell I was the only eleven-year-old boy inside the gym that night. There were some seventh graders, but everyone stood arranged in concentric rings, kind of like what you'd see around Saturn. Seventh-grade boys made up the outermost ring. They stood with their backs pressed up against the walls of the gym, holding plastic cups filled with diluted punch, watching what was taking place on the inside rings of kids, telling (excuse me) dumb jokes and making fun of people in the inner rings, but never being bold enough to detach themselves from the wall.

Seventh- and eighth-grade girls made up the middle rings. They were all dressed much nicer than any of the boys, and they kind of rocked and spun in place slightly, and talked to each other in small groups, pretending like they didn't care that a small number of kids were actually dancing.

The innermost ring was made up almost entirely of eighth-grade boys. They defined the limits of the actual dance floor, but not one of them looked like he would ever get out and dance. About half the rest of the eighth-grade boys were rogue asteroids who cut through the rings and burned their way past the dancers on urgent missions to get more food or carelessly bump into and intimidate smaller kids. It was like the asteroids *wanted* to "accidentally" cause some mass extinction event or something. James Jenkins was the biggest (excuse me) asteroid at the dance. The asteroids also mostly came with half-untucked shirts, they were in their socks (the permission slip explained that shoes were the only article of clothing we were allowed to remove), their mothers had clearly neither combed nor gelled their hair, and for whatever reason they tended to all be sweaty and smell bad.

I wondered if Coach Bovard was going to take the asteroids down below to the dungeon of the locker room and make them take showers before they could go home. Nobody likes to sit next to a sweaty, smelly eighth-grade boy, after all.

The bravest kids in space—a couple dozen of them, maybe—danced in the center of all the rings. About three-fourths of the dancers were girls. Nobody actually danced with anyone; they just twitched and avoided eye contact with other dancers, and especially with the rings. The boys who danced tried to be at the very nucleus of the mass, probably so that none of their friends could make fun of them.

It was horrifying, especially because there was no ring where I belonged.

Also, I was very mad at Karim for breaking up with Faye McMahon just so he could avoid being there at the (excuse me) dumb dance with me.

I tried to squeeze my way into the outer ring between a couple of the seventh-grade boys, but there was so little room against the wall, I started to feel anxious and claustrophobic. So I transformed into an asteroid and wove my way through the inner rings of girls until I got to the edge of the dance floor with the other eighth-grade boys. Then I saw Mr. Mannweiler and Coach Bovard in the middle of the dancers, making sure no contracts were being breached, and when Coach Bovard made eye contact with me I nearly fainted. I was convinced he deeply hated me for being the first boy of the year to break his absolutely-no-talking-in-the-locker-room rule.

The asteroid that had once been Sam Abernathy was collapsing and fizzling into a black hole. And Mom wouldn't be back to pick me up for hours.

If only I had a magnesium-flint fire starter and a knife with me, I would walk home and look for beer cans and a creek to live by for the rest of my life, I thought. Instead I decided to try the free punch and cookies.

The punch and cookies were both only slightly better than boiled creek water and crayfish. I looked around for a trash can to get rid of them in, hoping that time would somehow speed up—that we'd hit one of those bends Hayley Garcia (who was dancing in the center of Saturn) had told us about, and that this dance would end immediately, but no such luck.

Time was just unbending time.

I saw Karim's cousin Bahar, who was also not a part of any ring, near the trash can, getting rid of her punch and cookies as well.

"Oh. Hi, Sam," Bahar said.

Bahar was in eighth grade too. In fact, she was in my Algebra II class. She had always been nice to me, but I naturally assumed it was a political form of niceness, diplomatic, since she was my best friend's cousin and all. Like most people who'd known me ever since I was "the boy in the well"—the kid people everywhere were supposed to pray for—Bahar always made me feel embarrassed and small, which is exactly how I felt most of the time around everyone else anyway.

"Hi, Bahar," I said. I glanced over my shoulder toward the rings of Saturn, just to see if anyone might be making fun of her for talking to me.

"The cookies are terrible," Bahar said.

"Grocery store cookies. There's really no excuse for ever serving store cookies. And in the dark, raisins look like chocolate chips, which is another layer of disappointment on top of it," I pointed out.

That made Bahar laugh and nod. "Is Karim here? There's, like, no one to talk to. Everyone here is all caught up in either wanting to dance or wanting *not* to dance but looking like they do."

I shook my head. "Karim broke up with Faye McMahon just so he wouldn't have to come to the dance. So I guess Karim is champion of the not-dancing competition."

Bahar said, "That sounds like something Karim would do."

"I can't dance, anyway." I looked out to the pulsing center of

Saturn. It didn't look like anyone else could dance either, to be honest. I said, "I only came because my mom and dad *forced me* to come."

"Oh. Sorry about your parents making you come. I never would have thought of you as someone who'd get all dressed up and go out to a dance. My parents almost refused to allow me to come, after they read what the contract said."

"The—excuse me—sexually suggestive dancing and underwear rules?"

Bahar laughed. "Exactly. But at least *we're* having fun, right?"

I thought about it.

This was the first time since landing in Dick Dowling Middle School that anyone had ever been nice to me. But I reasoned it was just because of Karim—the whole diplomacy thing.

"Oh," I said, "I just love fixing up my hair and getting dressed up in a ridiculous outfit just so I can go somewhere and feel like I don't belong."

And Bahar said, "I think you look—"

But just then Bahar was cut off by a commotion of eighth-grade asteroids who came jettisoning out of the boys' bathroom, crazed with excitement. One of them laughed hysterically and yelled (excuse me), "Poop! Oh my God! Someone made a poop on the floor! It's as big as my leg!"

Welcome back to school, Mustangs!

This was a middle school dance.

And I imagined a new rule would inevitably show up in next year's dance contract.

NEVER CLIMB A T. REX IN A KILT

"It starts with mastering Biology, Sam."

My dad continued, advising me as he so frequently did, "That's how a kid like you can enter ninth grade at Blue Creek Magnet and go straight into their Advanced Placement Physics program!"

One of these days—maybe it would be on one of our survival campouts, maybe it would be over dinner, or it might even be on kilt day at the miniature golf course—Dad would just maybe, possibly by accident, ask me what I wanted to do about future things.

We were working at Lily Putt's Indoor-Outdoor Miniature Golf Course on Saturday, the day after the terrible dance. Dad liked to take advantage of slow times, like when I was cleaning up, to give me pep talks about his plans for me.

He also made me wear my kilt that day, so I came up with excuses to stay behind the counter at the snack bar, just in case any kids from Dick Dowling showed up.

Who was I kidding? Kids from Dick Dowling were there

pretty much all day on Saturdays, and hiding when you're a boy and also in Texas, and wearing a kilt, is impossible.

Still, on kilt days at the golf course, I always refused to climb up the volcano or the T. rex hole to dislodge any stuck balls. Climbing up anything as tall as our volcano or T. rex was far too dangerous in a kilt.

Along with a two-screen movie house and a diner called Colonel Jenkins's Diner, which was owned and operated by Kenny Jenkins (father of the murderer James Jenkins), our miniature golf course was the biggest attraction in Blue Creek. Actually, those were the only three attractions in Blue Creek, unless you included as *attractions* the three schools, a church, the post office, the creek, a stuffed calf at Blue Creek Feeds, and a few hundred homes and farms.

We inherited Lily Putt's Indoor-Outdoor Miniature Golf Course from my great-grandmother, whose name was Lily Abernathy. I never knew her, but she had been a very popular gospel singer, and even won a Grammy for a song called "I Will Walk with Him in the Garden of Blood."

Needless to say, my great-grandmother's song always made me think of James Jenkins.

As usual I wasn't enthusiastically listening to Dad about my future at Blue Creek Magnet High School. I was preparing a yogurt-and-mint sauce for the lamb burgers on psomi bread that were featured for the weekend in the snack bar.

So I said, "Sounds like a plan, Dad."

Our snack bar did a lot of business on weekends.

My dad looked puzzled. "Is something wrong?"

This was a potential breakthrough.

I inhaled deeply and looked up from the mint I was chopping. Finally, I had an opportunity to actually talk to my dad about what I wanted to do. At last I could tell Dad how much I hated living in Blue Creek, where I would always be THE LITTLE BOY IN THE WELL—the kid everyone was supposed to pray for. Finally, I could let Mom and Dad off the hook for all their planning—all their obsession about making sure I'd never have the freedom to fall into unseen holes in my future. And maybe doing so would free me from my quiet submission to never do something as foolish as fall into a hole and disappoint my parents ever again.

I said, "Yeah, Dad. I was . . . um . . . thinking about Blue Creek Magnet, and I—"

"No. I mean, where are Rigo and Maribel?" Dad asked.

Rigo and Maribel ran the golf course when we weren't there.

"Someone got some balls stuck in the T. rex," I said. "You know, I probably shouldn't climb up something like a T. rex with my kilt on, and all."

Dad laughed. "Ha ha! That's my boy! Heh. Maybe one day you'll invent an autonomous robot and program it to retrieve stuck golf balls!"

"In a kilt," I added. Then I pointed over to the main counter and said, "Dad, there's a line of people waiting to play."

COOK'S RIOT!

Sunday starts with a breakfast of negative feedback.

Once a week, on Sundays, the people of Blue Creek receive the *Hill Country Yodeler*, our local paper that mostly recycles stories about how people from out in the cities drive too dangerously through our town, how much rainfall we received during this month last year, and when the next Dumpster Day will be held at the community center.

Dumpster Days are opportunities for people to discard things like old refrigerators or transmissions—things that are too enormous to just leave out on the street for garbage collection, and that don't look good getting rusty piled up for years on the side of your house.

The other thing that is a regular feature in the *Yodeler* is a food column—a critique of local eating establishments—called Cook's Riot!

The column is written by James Jenkins's father, Kenny, who also owns and operates the only Blue Creek eatery, Colonel Jenkins's Diner.

Last summer, Kenny Jenkins devoted two complete months of his column to comparing and criticizing the different subtle successes and failures of the Whataburger locations in Taylor, Hutto, Pflugerville, Georgetown, Cedar Park, Bastrop, Giddings, and Lakeway. It was riveting stuff, for example, when Kenny Jenkins did such things as claim, "The green chile double in Pflugerville drips with despair and a Chernobyl-like afterbirth. If I saw one of these monstrosities in my yard at night, I would have no choice but to shoot it, and then burn down my house in an attempt to halt the spread of whatever contagion it undoubtedly transmits."

The main feature of Kenny Jenkins's column is the author's unswerving confidence in his expertise, and unapologetic cruelty to any dining establishment that is not his own.

Kenny Jenkins was a kind of celebrity in Blue Creek because of how intimidating and simultaneously classy he was, and also because he'd been on a Food Network cooking competition show, even though he was eliminated in the first round for serving a taco on an unheated corn tortilla.

Blue Creek normally did not have any celebrities unless it was late in the high school football season.

I got into my Clan Abernathy kilt and knee socks, pulled on a T-shirt, and went down to breakfast.

While Dad was getting into his kilt, and Mom hunted for his misplaced sporran, which is another name for "Scottish man purse," Dylan smeared scrambled eggs and ketchup in his hair, and my sister Evie poured herself a bowl of cereal, just as I opened up the *Yodeler* to read the latest installment of Kenny Jenkins's Cook's Riot!

I read the opening paragraph and stopped. Then I read it again to be sure I hadn't lost my mind.

This Sunday's Cook's Riot! column was about the food served at Lily Putt's Indoor-Outdoor Miniature Golf Course.

Kenny Jenkins wrote an entire column of nastiness about me, particularly about the food I prepare for the weekend menu at the golf course.

At Lily Putt's Snack Bar, one might endeavor to be daring and try the Lame (on-site, it is mislabeled "Lamb") Burger, which is served on a pair of roofing shingles that are on an apparent meandering journey through Blue Creek and traveling incognito as psomi bread. If that were not sufficient cause to make one consider expatriation from the planet, the yogurt-mint sauce, which tastes suspiciously of insecticide and acetone and finishes off with a flourish of hot asphalt, is bound to do the trick. The best course of action to pursue with one of Lily Putt's Lamb Burgers? Drive it out to a desolate portion of the panhandle, drop it off there, and pray it doesn't succeed in following you back home. You may want to bring a shovel, to bury it first as a precaution.

Mom and Dad told me it was great publicity for the golf course, despite my argument that there was no such thing as *publicity* in Blue Creek.

But I was confused. I should have been mad at Kenny Jenkins, but, oddly enough, I wasn't. The column just made me feel mopey and depressed about everything. I knew Kenny Jenkins was wrong about the food I made at Lily Putt's, and that he was just a mean, nasty person, but pointing that out to anyone would be like pointing out that Texas was a pretty big place, sizewise. The thing is, I could have just as easily penned a *publicity piece* about Colonel Jenkins's Diner—about how the restaurant used frozen *everything*, and liberally seasoned their output with two exclusive flavors, salt and margarine, but it would have been a waste of my energy. Everyone in Blue Creek knew Kenny Jenkins couldn't cook to save his life, but people still ate at his diner because being lazy about cooking a meal is the foundation of human nature, and people generally agreed that Kenny Jenkins's column was funny and acerbic. Also, just like I was with his son James, everyone in Blue Creek was afraid of Kenny Jenkins.

Mom drove Dad and me, in our kilts, into town to open up the golf course that morning.

She reached over the seat and patted my knee. It felt weird, being in essentially a skirt and all. I sat between Dylan and Evie and their car seats.

Mom said, "You're awfully quiet, Sam."

I just nodded and made eye contact with her in the rear-view mirror.

She said, "Well, don't feel bad, sweetie. Everyone adores the burgers you make."

Dad turned around and looked at me.

Dad said, "Don't take it too seriously, buddy. It's just food, after all. Making stuff like food, just to make people *happy*, is not worth getting all sensitive about. It's not like it'll change the world or make people's lives better—like designing some new kind of gadget that saves time and effort—maybe one that will automatically tune up your car while you're asleep or something. Wouldn't that be a great idea? You should write that down, so you remember it when you get to high school next year. The whole point of our campouts is to affirm to the world that all a man needs is a knife and some fire and he'll be perfectly fine, am I right? Kenny Jenkins can't criticize that, no matter what success and survival taste like!"

But I wasn't listening to Dad.

I was thinking up a way to prepare a crispy-pork-belly burger, and how I'd maybe serve it on a warm cornbread-inspired roll with a grilled-pineapple-and-mango salsa, and wondering if we had the right stuff for it in the kitchen at Lily Putt's.

THE
FIRST
NIGHT
IN
THE
HOLE

I WILL WALK WITH HIM IN THE GARDEN OF BLOOD

It all starts with pitch-darkness, singing, and cold rain.

People from all over had come to see the hole I'd fallen into. Above, they'd been pushed back behind a ribbon of plastic yellow caution tape. The rescuers were concerned that the weight of all those post-Thanksgiving-dinner Texans might affect the stability of the well.

A thick black cable was snaked down into the well. A white-hot light beamed from the end of it, and there was also some kind of speaker on it too, which is where my dad's voice came from.

"Sam? Sweetie, if you can hear me, can you please say something? Let us know you're okay? Can you see the light? We can't see you on the camera."

The cable with the light on it had gotten stuck on the same ledge I hit on my way down, about fifteen feet above me.

"Dad? I fell down here. I'm sorry for ruining Thanksgiving," I said.

My voice sounded gritty, like the dirt from the well had formed mud clots in my throat.

Then came the noise of dozens of people cheering above me. I didn't know why everyone was so happy; I was miserable.

"Sam? Where are you? Are you hurt? Does anything hurt, buddy?" my dad asked.

I turned my head to look around the bottom of the well. I saw a quarter and the cap off a plastic water bottle. In the light that shined from the end of the cable, I could fully see how filthy I was, and how confined the space around me was too. I looked for Bartleby, convinced that he was about to play a trick on everyone and laugh at us for being fools, but he was gone. It kind of made me mad to think that Bartleby had abandoned me, after what I'd put up with from him.

What a coward, I thought.

My dad's voice echoed again, "Can you move your hands and feet?"

Of course I could move my hands and feet, I thought. I'd just crawled through a tunnel to Ethan Pixler's coffin and back.

I wiggled my hands and feet.

"I don't think I'm hurt, Dad. I'm just stuck, is all."

I started crying. I couldn't help it.

Above me, the cheering got very quiet.

But something cold and wet began dripping on my legs. And I got really mad at first because I thought it was Bartleby making (excuse me) "unicorn pee," but it turned out to be only rain, which was probably worse. And as the rain fell, and the bottom of the well transformed into a cold pudding of mud, my father reassured me they were in the process of putting up a tent to stop the runoff from coming down the hole, while the other people who were waiting up above for some kind of miracle—perhaps me or Ethan Pixler to rise up and thank them for being so kind and waiting in the rain for something miraculous to happen—began to sing.

They sang my great-grandmother's song, "I Will Walk with Him in the Garden of Blood."

> *On my passing I will walk in a garden*
> *Awash with the blood that grants heaven's pardon.*
> *A fragrant rose from ev'ry sin I've committed*
> *Will bloom and sing out, "This sinner's been acquitted."*

Unlike "Deep in the Heart of Texas"—where you get to clap and stuff—it was not a very cheerful song.

I knew every word, too, but nothing about my great-grandmother's Grammy-winning gospel song made the first bit of sense to me at four years old. But if armadillos could talk, I suppose blood-soaked roses could sing.

Then my dad said, "Sam? Just hang in there, buddy. We're going to get you out of there. Just try to stay calm."

I tried being calm, but nobody up there could possibly understand what it felt like to be down here. The muddy water was cold, and I couldn't raise myself up out of it.

I said, "I want to go home."

"We'll get you, Sam. Just breathe easy. The fire department is here, and the TV news came out, all the way from Austin. You should see what it looks like up here, Sam. There must be two hundred people out here praying for you," Dad said. "Can you see where the light is coming from?"

That sounded like the title to a gospel song, I thought. Maybe one where you could clap, or at least maybe snap your fingers or do arm movements, like the Chicken Dance.

The flow of water down the well slowed to a trickle and then finally stopped. They must have gotten the tent up to cover the hole, because I could still hear the drumming of dime-size Texas raindrops marching like a military parade on the canopy above, but I was still soaked and muddy. And trapped.

People were singing again.

I said, "The light's stuck on a rock or something, up above me pretty far. I can't reach it."

And that sounded like a gospel song too, I thought. Great-Grandma Lily Abernathy must have had an easy source of inspiration here in Texas.

Dad said, "That's okay, buddy. You just relax and stay still. We're working on it. We'll have you out in no time."

I had no choice but to stay still.

I heard my mother. She must have been standing right next to Dad. She was crying, and it made me feel terrible. It was all my fault. If I ever got out, I swore I would never do anything to disappoint Mom and Dad ever again.

Remembering this time, I suppose that up above me Mom and Dad were also determining how they would never again let me out of their sight long enough to fall into another hole. And that's pretty much the explanation of my life, when I think about it now. I wasn't going to disappoint them, and they weren't going to let me have that opportunity, not ever again.

I rested my head against the side of the well, shut my eyes, and tried to go to sleep.

FINDING A CHOCOLATE *YOU*

Then it starts with a discussion on aging.

Bartleby had come back.

I cannot say whether or not his return cheered me up. I was beginning to believe that things would work out just fine without him.

It must have been very late. There is a certain kind of quiet that only happens around two o'clock in the morning—and that was exactly the kind of quiet that had settled down, covering me like a thick blanket inside my well.

The light was still shining at the end of the rescue cable, and the rain continued its patter against the tent above the hole, but the singing had stopped. There were no sounds coming down the well at all from the people who'd been gathered earlier.

I figured whoever had been up above me had all decided to go to bed and get a fresh, dry start in the morning, and maybe eat leftovers too.

My stomach growled.

"I like mud," Bartleby said. "I think mud is the best way to get soft, youthful-looking skin. It's the most effective method for reversing the aging process, if you ask me."

I did not ask Bartleby.

Also, there was so much mud on my face that my eyes had been crusted shut. I felt them crack apart like dried tempera paint when I opened them. And there was Bartleby, right in front of me, his whiskered snout so close to my own nose that the bristles on his face tickled me.

Somehow, Bartleby had managed to smear mud all over his face too.

He looked ridiculous.

I must have looked like a pond catfish trapped in slop during the final stages of a drought.

"Thanks for leaving me," I said as sarcastically as I could manage, which was not very sarcastic at all, considering I was not that kind of commentator.

Bartleby flicked his snout up in the direction of the light.

"I'm camera shy," he explained. "I can't deal with crowds of people. They don't *get me*. But look at you, Sam! You look like a chocolate bunny! Well, except for the ears and maybe the tail. But besides that, looking at you makes me think of one thing—finding a chocolate *you* in my basket on Easter morning!"

The thought of Bartleby eating me—even a chocolate version of me—was somewhat disturbing.

"So now you're going to tell me that armadillos get Easter baskets too," I said.

Bartleby shook his head. "You're such a negative little chocolate boy," he said. "You should embrace the fact that the world has many more pleasant things than you're probably capable of realizing, Sam."

But Bartleby was right: I *was* negative, and I *was* covered in mud. Completely. It felt awful—all that wet grit inside my clothes, everywhere. Somehow, the sock on my shoeless foot had come off, and I thought, now Mom and Dad were *really* going to be disappointed with me for falling into a hole *and* losing one of my socks.

Bartleby took a deep breath and exhaled a satisfied sigh. "Mud. It's so nice!"

"It's awful," I said.

Bartleby said, "Negative again. You'll never age if you have a positive attitude and take regular mud baths. Trust me."

"But I want to age. I want to grow up," I said.

"Nonsense! What's the good in it?" Bartleby asked.

"Well, to begin with, if I grow up, I will probably be too big to fall into small holes. And I will also not make my parents feel disappointed in me."

Bartleby scratched his muddy beard with an equally muddy claw. He said, "If all you ever want to do in life is *not disappoint* people, well . . . where does that leave you, Sam?"

I honestly couldn't say where it left me. Bartleby was so

ANDREW SMITH

annoying, though—especially when he made me *think* about things.

"But I ruined their Thanksgiving. I probably ruined their lives by falling down here," I said, starting to feel a little weepy under all my mud once again.

"Listen—I'll tell you a trick," Bartleby said. "But you have to keep it secret."

"What trick?"

"It's about trying to *not disappoint* people." When Bartleby said "not disappoint," he made air quotes with his front claws. Then he went on. "What you really need to do is at the heart of any con game: You have to make people *want to* give you what you want to steal from them, without ever asking them for it."

"I don't know what you're talking about," I said.

"One day you will," Bartleby said. "If other people are going to spend their lives trying to make you never fall into holes, and all you want to do is *not disappoint* them, trick them into handing over what you think they want to protect themselves from. Just like I did, when I made you ask me to prove I was a unicorn, when in fact I am the Armadillo of Thanksgiving Present. Ha ha!"

I didn't really get what Bartleby meant; I wouldn't get it for a number of years, in fact. But just thinking about not falling into holes, and Mom and Dad trying to save me from every hole that could ever show up in my path, made me feel sad and helpless.

"Guess how old I am," Bartleby said.

I looked at Bartleby's muddy, vacuum-cleaner-shaped armadillo face.

"Go on, guess," Bartleby prodded.

When I didn't say anything to him, Bartleby began uttering a constant, rhythmic stream of "Guess . . . Guess . . . Guess . . ."

Bartleby's ability to annoy was tireless.

After what seemed like an hour and a half of his endless "Guess . . . Guess . . . Guess . . ." I finally gave in.

I had no idea how old armadillos could possibly be. I figured they lived as long as houseplants.

"Two," I guessed.

Bartleby exploded in laughter. "Ha ha! Wrong! See? I told you, it's the mud!" Then he stroked the side of his snout lovingly with a claw and said, "So youthful! So pretty!"

If I could have folded my arms across my chest and rolled away from Bartleby, I would have. But I had to stay on my back in order to keep my face out of the mud I was lying in.

"Well, how old are you, then?" I asked.

"Eh. How would I know?" Bartleby said. "Besides, unicorns live forever. Anyhow, come on. There's something else I want to show you down here."

Bartleby turned and receded inside his tunnel once again.

I did not want to follow him.

"Come on," Bartleby said.

I stayed.

"Come on."

Nothing.

"Follow me."

He waited, and after I did not respond, Bartleby said, "Follow me. Follow me. Follow me. Follow me."

I said nothing.

"Follow me."

He was so annoying.

"Follow me."

And, after I waited a few minutes in silence, from the mouth of Bartleby's tunnel came his voice: "Sam?"

"What?" I said.

"Guess how old I am. Ha ha! Just kidding! Follow me."

"No. There are people up there who are trying to help me," I said.

Bartleby curled his body around and poked his muddy face at me.

"Don't worry. They're going to take at least another whole day. Trust me—I saw what they're doing. They're digging a side tunnel." And then Bartleby swept his front claw in a slow-motion diagonal karate chop and added, "On an *angle*."

Bartleby's black armadillo eyes got wider when he said it.

I didn't care about any of that. There was only one thing that Bartleby said that stuck in my head. "I have to stay here a *whole extra day*?"

"That's why you should follow me!" Bartleby said. "I'll get

you back in time for everyone to feel like heroes."

"Wait. Have you been up there? On the outside?"

Bartleby paused for a moment. He looked from side to side, thinking. Then he said, "Of course I haven't gone up there, Sam."

So I was convinced I'd caught Bartleby in a lie, which in retrospect was not much of an accomplishment, considering he never told the truth. "How else would you know they're digging a side tunnel?" I asked.

Bartleby added, "*On an angle.*"

And again Bartleby did the slow-motion diagonal karate chop and widened his beady black eyes. Then he made a grimacing smile, baring his pointy little armadillo teeth.

Bartleby turned his snout back into his tunnel and said, "Follow me."

I WILL NEVER *NOT BE* THE LITTLE BOY IN THE WELL

This starts with a secret hideout.

I followed Bartleby back into his network of tunnels.

Up above, a well-digging crew had plotted out a method for excavating a rescue shaft—*on an angle*—that would intersect with my abandoned well just where I had been trapped, at the muddy bottom. Digging progressed very slowly.

During the night, the story of Blue Creek's "Boy in the Well" was told and retold on every news channel in the country. They used a photo of me as a three-year-old, swimming at a hotel pool in Austin, which was totally embarrassing because I was shirtless *and* had inflatable floaties on my biceps.

That night, someone began selling PRAY FOR SAM shirts on the Internet.

In less than twelve hours, my life in Blue Creek had been forever doomed, written out like the script of a movie I hadn't yet seen.

Up until that Thanksgiving Day when I played Spud with Karim and some neighborhood kids, when James Jenkins threw the ball higher than anyone thought he could throw it, Blue

Creek was only known for a few reasonably forgettable things: my great-grandmother Lily Abernathy's Grammy-winning gospel song, "I Will Walk with Him in the Garden of Blood"; Lily Putt's Indoor-Outdoor Miniature Golf Course (with its bottomless root beer and black-light rock-'n'-roll indoor golf parties for teens every Friday and Saturday night); Colonel Jenkins's Diner's chicken-fried steak on a stick; and a moth-eaten stuffed two-headed calf that stood behind the counter at Blue Creek Feeds.

Now Blue Creek would never *not be* the town at the epicenter of "Pray for Sam" and "The Little Boy in the Well." Other parts of the country had relatively short memories when it came to such things, but small towns in Texas that stake a claim to fame never forget what it was that put them on the map.

And as long as I lived in Blue Creek, Texas, I would never *not be* Sam Abernathy, the Little Boy in the Well, the floatie-wearing shirtless kid everyone was supposed to pray for.

Thump.

For a moment I thought Bartleby had run into Ethan Pixler's coffin again, but this was a deeper, heavier sound.

"Ah! Found it!" Bartleby said.

Then came the distinctive squeak of a metal hinge, and the creaky complaint of an ancient door swinging open.

"You're not opening the coffin, are you?" I said.

"Ha ha! No! It's not a coffin; it's a door! A door to a pot of gold! Come on, follow me!" Bartleby said.

I followed Bartleby through a tiny arched doorway. It didn't make any sense, really—what was a door doing way down here, and why was it so small? The only thing a door like this might be used for would be cats, or maybe leprechauns. Or talking armadillos and four-year-old boys who were covered in mud.

But once I'd passed through the doorway, I realized it wasn't that small after all—that most of it was covered up by dirt, so Bartleby and I crawled through just the upper few inches of what was a regular-size doorway, into what turned out to be a regular-size room.

I could even stand up in it.

Well, I could *try* to stand up, but my legs were too wobbly and sore from me being trapped in the well, so I ended up sitting down on the dusty floor of a long-abandoned cellar.

"Well? What do you think?" Bartleby asked.

I didn't really know what I was supposed to think. The place was old, dusty, and creepy. Tree roots hung like wild frizzy hair from the ceiling, and the floor was covered with a thick layer of ashy dust and cobwebs. There were two upended chairs, one of them missing two of its legs, a card table, a dresser with all the drawers pulled halfway out, and some empty mason jars scattered across the floor. In the middle of the room squatted an old iron stove, its chimney pipe disconnected and hanging down from the ceiling like a permanently astonished mouth saying, "Ooooooh!"

One of the dresser drawers was filled with buttons, nickels, and pennies. This turned out to be Bartleby's "pot of gold," which was obviously quite worthless. In another drawer I found some playing cards and a small poster that was printed by the Milam County

Board of Health. The poster was all about keeping flies and mosquitos away from babies, and how you should never show off a baby to strangers if you want your baby to grow up and be happy.

I figured when they printed the poster, they must not have had things like cable television and abandoned wells, and cameras on the end of rescue cables and so on.

"Your pot of gold is a box of buttons and change, and now I suppose you're going to tell me this is where we'll find the Ghost of Thanksgiving Future," I said.

"Ha ha! Good one, Sam!" Bartleby shook his pointy head. "There's a surprise, though! A surprise in your future—trust me! But your future is going to be a hungry one. Sorry to say I already ate all the food that was left in here. If it's any consolation, it didn't taste that good."

I didn't really think I wanted food that was buried in an abandoned cellar anyway.

And Bartleby went on, as usual. "Welcome to Ethan Pixler's secret hideout! And I bet you're wondering why Ethan Pixler needed a secret hideout. Well, it's because Ethan Pixler was a bank robber, which explains the pot of gold, and the whole, you know—*tchk!*"

And when Bartleby made the *tchk!* sound, he pulled an imaginary rope with his claw from the side of his neck and stuck his tongue out from the corner of his narrow mouth, dramatizing the end of Ethan Pixler's bank robbery career for me.

Bartleby cleared his throat and spit a wad of muddy armadillo saliva onto Ethan Pixler's secret hideout's floor. He said,

"Well, I guess it's not so secret now. You know about it, and so do I, and so do a few thousand of my friends, I suppose. But don't tell anyone. The pot of gold belongs to *me*."

That was when I really suspected Bartleby was a delusional liar. The pot of gold was worthless, and there was no way Bartleby could possibly have thousands of friends. Or any, for that matter.

"Judging by his loot, Ethan Pixler was not good at picking banks to rob, and judging by his coffin, Ethan Pixler wasn't super good at secretly hiding, either," I said.

Bartleby nodded thoughtfully. "When it comes to choosing a secret hiding spot, you can only be wrong once."

But Bartleby apologized for the condition of Ethan Pixler's secret hideout, and for the fact that we couldn't play cards since the deck that had been left behind by Ethan Pixler's gang only had forty-nine cards in it, and also because Bartleby's claws made it too difficult for him to hold a hand of cards without me seeing what he had. And then Bartleby accused me of being a card cheater in waiting, and he got mad at me and said that he didn't want to talk to me anymore, which would have been fine with me even though I knew there was nothing that could ever make Bartleby stop talking.

Not ever.

Because, naturally, Bartleby waved a crusty claw in the air and announced, "Aha! Right on time!"

Of course, I had no idea what Bartleby was talking about, but almost as soon as he said it, something black and jiggling came floating down from the black mouth of the stove's disconnected chimney pipe. It looked like a nervous cloud of smoke or something, and it was immediately followed by more floating blobs—more and more of them—until all around us, everywhere, the air in Ethan Pixler's secret hideout was alive and buzzing with thousands and thousands of pairs of fluttering silky wings.

The room was filling up with bats.

"My friends! My friends! Ha ha! Isn't this great?" Bartleby squealed. "I told you! I have thousands of friends! I have the biggest friends list in Texas! This is so great!"

Bartleby fluttered his claws and hopped, dancelike, from hind foot to hind foot.

I did not think it was great. In fact, to me, bats were about as appealing as flying snakes. Their wings rubbed noiselessly all over my muddy clothes and in my hair. I sank low against the floor of the hideout, nearly convinced that if I breathed too hard, I might actually inhale an entire living bat.

Within minutes the tornado of bats stilled and every available inch of surface on the walls and ceiling of the hideout was covered by the tiny quivering creatures. And each one of the bats seemed to have its eyes pinned on Bartleby and me.

"Is this the Little Boy in the Well?" the bats asked. They all spoke in the most absolutely disciplined chorus. Every one of them exact.

"Ha ha!" Bartleby laughed and waved his front claws. He attempted to clap, but armadillo arms being what they are, they produced only a feeble kind of *click! click!* sound.

"Yes! This is Sam Abernathy, Pray for Sam, the Little Boy in the Well!" Bartleby said.

"He doesn't look like his picture. This one's chubby, and dirty," the bats, who had obviously seen me on television, said.

I didn't really know what I looked like, but I was aware that I was completely covered in mud, and also a bit bigger than three-year-old Sam Abernathy. But I was definitely *not chubby*.

"I am not chubby!" I argued.

"You are very chubby," the bats replied. "Especially compared with the picture of the boy who had the orange balloons on his arms."

I knew a few things about bats, living in the region of Texas where Blue Creek was, but I never knew bats paid attention to cable television. Or that they talked.

"And why do the bats all say exactly the same thing, at exactly the same time?" I whispered to Bartleby.

"Ha ha! Yes! They're *social animals*," Bartleby said. And when he said "social animals" he made air quotes with his hooked front claws and widened his eyes, which was Bartleby's default expression for dramatic emphasis. "They're just like human beings. Ha ha! They all say exactly the same thing, without even thinking about it, at exactly the same time! Ha ha!"

A few more straggler bats squeezed out from the chimney pipe and wedged themselves into place between the others on the walls, or hung themselves by their little feet from the roots sticking out of the ceiling.

But one thing I did know about bats is that they always

went back to their home when the sun came up.

It was the morning of my second day in the well, and people would be working at getting me out. I needed to get back to my place—what if Dad and Mom were trying to talk to me?

I climbed up the wall of dirt that lay blocking most of the doorway and stuck my head into the small passageway where Bartleby and I had entered Ethan Pixler's secret hideout.

"Hey! Where are you going?" Bartleby said.

"Hey! Where are you going?" echoed the ten thousand bats in the hideout.

"It's morning," I said. "I have to get back. What if they think something happened to me?"

I squeezed my way through the tiny doorway, and Bartleby said, "I'm pretty sure everyone in the world knows something happened to you, Sam."

And the bats said, "Everyone in the world knows."

I pulled myself back through Bartleby's tunnel in the direction of the well.

Bartleby called after me, "Sam? Wait a second. Sam?"

"Wait a second, Sam," said the thousands of bats.

And ahead of me I could hear my father's voice echoing through the metallic buzz of the speaker on the rescue cable that had been inserted into the opening of the well. He said, "Sam? Are you awake, sweetie? We're almost there, buddy. Hang in there. Sam? Sam? Can you hear me?"

"Sam? Can you hear me?" said the bats.

ANDREW SMITH

EIGHTH
GRADE

MY AFTER-SCHOOL HOMEWORK BUDDY

This starts a few weeks after the dance, at Colonel Jenkins's Diner.

When the first progress marks were assigned at Dick Dowling Middle School, Mom and Dad announced they would reward me by taking us all out to dinner. I was getting straight As (except for PE, where I had a B, along with a comment that accused me of talking too much). The problem is that "out to dinner" to me means going somewhere that *does not* serve chicken-fried steak on a stick (with a plastic half-cup container of gravylike substance to dip it in).

And while I did momentarily fantasize about *salade Niçoise*, given that we lived in Blue Creek I realistically understood deep down what "going out" would actually involve, which meant only one thing: Colonel Jenkins's.

The diner smelled like floor wax and the interior of an old school bus. Everything was plastic—the tables, the booths, even the cutlery you were given with your meal, which had to be ordered and picked up (something that was completely barbaric, if you ask me) at the plastic counter. There was also quite probably a high plastic content in the food Kenny Jenkins served at his diner too. Every newspaper column from Kenny Jenkins's Cook's Riot! had been clipped from the *Hill Country Yodeler*, matted, framed, and hung on the walls. When we went inside, I scanned the frames for the column about my hamburgers but couldn't find it. I did see the almost shrinelike display of the entire front page from the *Yodeler* from seven years ago—the one with the banner headline:

BLUE CREEK'S MIRACLE BOY!

"Oh my gosh! Look how tall you've gotten, Jimmy!" Dad practically erupted with hot volcanic glee when he saw James Jenkins taking orders at the counter, dressed in a ketchup-stained white apron and a paper waiter's hat with a blue stripe along its side.

I kind of shrank back behind Mom and Dad. Spending every day in two classes with James Jenkins—one of them being the cruel gladiatorial contest of Boys' PE—I saw him entirely too frequently for my comfort.

Also, James Jenkins hated being called Jimmy. If Dad were in eighth grade, or possibly if he had been alone here, I was fairly certain James Jenkins would have punched my dad in the eye for calling him *Jimmy*.

And James Jenkins, who was clearly wearing a red-and-white engraved plastic name badge that said JAMES, didn't react. He didn't blink. He just stared straight ahead like he could see through us, not moving his head in any direction. Like a murderer. He held a pencil, its point pressed at a rigid forty-five-degree angle to the order pad on the counter, as though to tell us, *I do not want to say "Welcome to Colonel Jenkins's Diner. May I take your order, please?" So just tell me what you want and then run for your lives.*

"My, my!" Mom said. "It seems like only yesterday when you were just a baby, running around the neighborhood barefoot and in a soggy diaper! You must be in high school now, right, Jimmy?"

I thought for sure James Jenkins wanted to kill us all after that.

I felt like every time Mom or Dad said "Jimmy," and especially after the comment about the soggy diaper, James Jenkins was compounding the consequences he would eventually inflict on me. Also, Mom and Dad had NO CLUE that James Jenkins had been held back and was now in THE SAME GRADE as me despite the fact that he was practically A GROWN MAN. It was a story the editors of the *Hill Country Yodeler* must have somehow overlooked.

"I'm in eighth grade, Mrs. Abernathy," James said. He moved the point of the pencil about one-tenth of an inch, which is something a murderer would probably do. Then he added, "I'm in two of the same classes with *him*."

And when James Jenkins said "him," he moved his eyes (but not his chin) a quarter of an inch in my direction.

Dad lit up like a volcano of happiness on a moonless night. He said, "You're in some of Sam's classes? Maybe you boys can schedule a few after-school homework meet-ups sometime!"

(Excuse me.)

I counted—slowly, like James Jenkins would—to fifty-eight during the painful gap of silence that followed Dad's "after-school homework meet-ups" suggestion. James Jenkins didn't move; he didn't blink. Then finally, James Jenkins inhaled (slowly, like a murderer) through his nose and said this: "Maybe."

Then he moved his eyes a quarter inch again and looked at me.

GIFTED WITH A VISION OF MY FUTURE

It starts during dinner.

For whatever reasons, Dad decided to order Colonel Jenkins's World Famous Mac and Cheese Dogs and okra fries for everyone.

And for whatever reasons, at some point in his life Kenny Jenkins, who was James Jenkins's father, had come to the conclusion that putting macaroni and cheese on a hot dog with sweet relish was a clever idea. Maybe it was an old family recipe, handed down from the original Colonel Jenkins, who happened to enjoy prison food.

Dylan and Evie put extra ketchup on theirs.

While we ate, James Jenkins stood motionless at the counter. He may have been watching us, or he may have been in a state of suspended animation; I couldn't tell. Kenny Jenkins also watched us, from back in the kitchen where he was busily committing crimes against things that people eat. In fact, I thought that would be a real cracker of a line for the sarcastic review of the food at Colonel Jenkins's Diner I was imagining writing when I got home.

Dad shook his head and grinned. He had some cheese on his cheek.

Dad said (excuse me), "Dang! That Jimmy Jenkins is going to be some quarterback when he gets into the high school program. Just look at him! He must be six-one already. Maybe six-two! In eighth grade!"

And Mom, not paying attention to Dad, said something like, "Oh! This looks like it could be fun!"

Evie said something about not liking the okra fries, and Dylan, who at three didn't strive to be coherent, said, "Ketchup magnet!"

Dylan also poked an okra up his nose.

I ignored them all. I was too busy writing imaginary mean things about Kenny Jenkins and his (excuse me) dumb food.

Dad went on. "That's what everyone says around Blue Creek—that Kenny Jenkins has big plans for that boy's future in football. Makes sense, right?"

Blue Creek, Texas, was like the Promised Land for dads who made unilateral plans for their sons' lives.

Dad nodded to himself and agreed. "Makes sense."

I was concentrating on a metaphor that described the cheese sauce as something responsible for the extinction of the dinosaurs. It wasn't perfect, but I was working on it.

Dad went on, "Hey, Sammy, since he's in your class and all, maybe we could invite Jimmy to tag along on our next survival campout!"

I had a hard time imagining anything more terrifying. So I ignored Dad.

And Mom said to Dad, "I think I should try this. Don't you think, Dave?"

Dad, who thought Mom was involved in *his* conversation, said, "I've said it ever since I first saw that boy. That kid's a monster."

Yes, Dad, I thought, *he is*.

Mom shifted her paper placemat a quarter turn and pointed down at it. She said, "No. I'm talking about this."

Dylan had completed his mission: There were two okra fries in his nose.

Then Dad and I saw what Mom had been talking about. Our placemats were advertisements for Blue Creek Days, the annual town fair that celebrated everything there was to celebrate about the history of Blue Creek, Texas.

They didn't really need more than one day for Blue Creek Days.

We always avoided Blue Creek Days, which regularly featured a Little Boy in the Well attraction.

In a corner of the placemat, inside a box with stars for borders, was an announcement for the first-ever Blue Creek Days Colonel Jenkins Macaroni and Cheese Cook-Off Challenge. It encouraged all the citizens of Blue Creek to attempt to take on Kenny Jenkins in a contest to determine who could make the best macaroni and cheese dish in all of Texas.

The bottom lines of the announcement said this:

FIRST PLACE PRIZE: $500
Entries will be judged by Resa O'Hare, celebrity
chef and Culinary Arts instructor at Pine Mountain
Academy, home of one of America's leading culinary
programs for high school students!

And just like that I had been gifted with a vision of my future while I sat in front of a plastic foam plate full of Texas diner food at Colonel Jenkins's.

I had to do this.

Dad adjusted his bifocals and read the announcement.

He looked warily at me, then at Mom.

"Well, I bet you *could* do this, honey!" Dad was gushing again, but this time at Mom, as opposed to James Jenkins. Then he got a wicked look on his face and said, "But wait. Don't you have to know how to *cook* to enter this? Ha ha ha ha!" And he jokingly shoved my mom's shoulder, which almost made her fall out of her plastic chair, but she laughed too. Sort of.

I took a gulp of sweet tea to knock back the knot in my throat and said, "I'd like to enter this, Dad. I bet I could win."

For just a second Dad looked like I'd just told him the beautiful beer can he'd found had holes in the bottom of it, and then an Oh-I-figured-it-out smile stretched across his cheesy face and he laughed. "Ha ha ha! Good one, Sam!"

He thought I was joking.

Then Mom laughed too.

Dylan ate one of the okras from his nose.

Evie asked why everyone was laughing.

And Dad patted her ketchup-smeared hand and said, "Everyone in Blue Creek knows boys aren't supposed to cook, Evie. Not unless it's a matter of survival. Ha ha!"

And when Dad said "survival," his eyes got wide and dreamy, like he was revealing one of the deepest, most closely guarded secrets of life.

I caught Kenny Jenkins staring at us from back in the kitchen. Whatever. He was probably thinking about Lamb Burger Boy or Well Boy or maybe Blue Creek's Miracle Boy.

But before we left, I asked James Jenkins to give me an entry form for the contest. I folded it up and stuck it in my pocket, and when Dad asked what I'd been talking to James Jenkins about, I (excuse me) lied and told him we were talking about homework and football, and survival campouts.

Dad was so happy.

PLASTIC BOTTLES, ABANDONED WELLS, ALIENS, AND WORM FARMS

We start on Wednesday after school, at Science Club.

Science Club was the second-most popular club at Dick Dowling Middle School, just behind "Mathletes"—the competition mathematics club. Everyone (well, kids who liked math, at least) wanted to be a Mathlete because the kids in that club wore special jackets that looked like lettermen's jackets, only with a π symbol, as opposed to the uppercase double *D*s for Dick Dowling.

It was like all the grown-ups in Blue Creek had decided that if their kids weren't good enough to become Dallas Cowboys, they'd be happy in life as scientists or mathematicians. I figured if those plans didn't work out, most dads in Blue Creek would be okay with their kids living in the woods and foraging for beer cans and crawdads, or panhandling from hiking college students.

I didn't even know half the kids in Science Club. Like everything else in my post-four-year-old life, Mom and Dad signed me up for it without asking if I wanted to join. Karim was in the club, just because I was in it. And his cousin Bahar was in it too. But she liked science just about as much as anyone in Blue Creek liked Colonel Jenkins's World Famous Mac and Cheese Dogs, which, generally speaking, was a lot.

This Wednesday, the club was embroiled in a heated debate over our project display for Blue Creek Days. Karim was lobbying for building a papyrus reed boat from plastic water bottles, and then using it to catch the Loop Current in the Gulf of Mexico so we could sail across the Atlantic.

"That's dumb," Hayley Garcia, who was president of the club, said. "What if we didn't get the boat back in time to display it for Blue Creek Days?"

I didn't say anything, but I was actually thinking, What if it sank and we all died?

And: How would we get our water boiled?

And: There is NOTHING I would like to do LESS than to try to cross the Atlantic in a boat made from plastic bottles.

Science Club met in my homeroom—Mr. Mannweiler's classroom, since Mr. Mannweiler was also the Biology teacher at Dick Dowling Middle School. And although my dad insisted that I excel in Biology in order to get into AP Physics in high school, he didn't realize that one of the things Mr. Mannweiler made us do in class was to individually recite a memorized list of "The Twenty-Five Biology Terms Eighth-Grade Boys Cannot Say Without Laughing" until none of us laughed.

(Excuse me.)

That ordeal was worse than setting sail in a bunch of bottles from the garbage.

No boy *ever* wants to say those words in front of a bunch of other boys, much less in front of his homeroom teacher who happens to be a *man*.

Naturally, James Jenkins resisted being forced to say those words without sounding like a murderer, which made all the other boys laugh, so James Jenkins happened to be in after-school detention in the same room where we were meeting. James Jenkins was definitely *not* a Science Club–type guy. Not that I was either. And, also naturally, James Jenkins felt compelled to say something that he decided was important to our club.

James Jenkins raised his hand, very slowly, and then he just stared at Hayley Garcia without moving his head for about five minutes until she figured out that he wanted to say something to *her*, as opposed to asking Mr. Mannweiler if he could go to the (excuse me) restroom or something.

"What? What do you want, James?" Hayley Garcia, who was not the most patient science-loving Mustang at Dick Dowling, said.

"Maybe your display could be all about how it's possible for a human being to survive inside an abandoned well for three days," James suggested. "You could dig a hole and everything."

I sank down in my chair.

Hayley Garcia actually had a look on her face that implied

she was thinking about the merits of James Jenkins's idea.

Karim shook his head and (excuse me) whispered to me, "What a d-word."

And while Hayley Garcia stared at me as though she were calculating the exact size of the hole the club's members would have to dig, and as I was beginning to feel sweaty, claustrophobic, and sick, Bahar steered the garbage-bottle ship of Science Club back toward sanity by suggesting she thought Hayley's original idea—the one involving the detection and interpretation of low-frequency radio broadcasts as possible extraterrestrial communications signals using repurposed computers and shortwave radios from the 1940s—was the best idea proposed.

And Karim immediately seconded Bahar's endorsement. I found out later that Karim asked Hayley Garcia if she wanted to go steady, and she said yes, which I couldn't understand on account of Karim being only in sixth grade, but then again, I didn't understand virtually *anything* about middle school to begin with.

The approval of Hayley's low-frequency extraterrestrial idea made one of the club members—a kid named Michael Dolgoff—very disappointed. Michael Dolgoff wanted to build an arena and force black widow spiders to fight against potato bugs and night crawlers, and stuff like that. He wanted to call the display "Ultimate Natural Selection."

Michael Dolgoff's father owned a business called Fat Mike's Worm Farm. Michael Dolgoff's father sold bait.

(Excuse me.) "Science Club sucks," Michael Dolgoff said.

I kind of agreed with Michael Dolgoff, but I was tremendously relieved that nobody present was seriously thinking about burying me again. Except for maybe James Jenkins, but he didn't count since he was not officially in the club. But Hayley Garcia should never have allowed him to make a suggestion in the first place.

To be honest, I wouldn't have minded watching bugs fight in an arena, though, as long as I didn't have to touch them.

And I would have given James Jenkins a dirty look, but I was afraid of him. Besides, I had the filled-out entry form for the first-ever Blue Creek Days Colonel Jenkins Macaroni and Cheese Cook-Off Challenge in my pocket, and having James here with us in Mr. Mannweiler's room gave me an opportunity to hand it to him so I could avoid walking into Colonel Jenkins's Diner alone, and possibly having to face Kenny Jenkins one-on-one.

So I waited until the meeting wound down and Hayley Garcia listed all these decisions that the group had allegedly come to consensus on regarding our project display for Blue Creek Days. I wasn't really listening to her, because I was mad about the whole how-long-can-a-boy-survive-in-a-well thing, and I was also scared about giving my entry form to James Jenkins, which would require having to initiate a conversation with him, something I had never done since that Thanksgiving Day when I was four and James Jenkins basically tried to murder me. But the Science Club made some kind of plan involving radio stations, old computers, hostile extraterrestrials, and finding the highest point in Blue Creek.

I figured I'd catch up on it later; or maybe not. I didn't really care. There was only one thing I wanted to do at Blue Creek Days, and it didn't have anything to do with outer space.

PROJECT: ENTRY

It starts with me slipping a folded-in-fourths piece of paper across James Jenkins's detention desk.

James Jenkins didn't move. He didn't blink.

"What is this, Well Boy?" James said.

Karim and Bahar were waiting for me by the door. We always walked home together after Science Club. This time, Hayley Garcia, who was suddenly Karim's newest girlfriend, waited too. I was still unsure if I approved of Hayley Garcia, now especially because I was certain she actually thought putting me inside an empty well for three days was a good idea.

I glanced over at them.

Karim and Hayley were sending each other text messages on their cell phones and laughing about them, even though they were standing about eighteen inches away from each other.

What would extraterrestrials think of such behavior?

During school, kids got in trouble for having cell phones out. After Science Club, there really were no rules—just like Ultimate Natural Selection.

Bahar looked at her cousin and rolled her eyes at me.

"Um," I said.

I'll admit it: I really did not know how anyone like me could ever speak to anyone like James Jenkins.

I swallowed and asked him, "Could you please give that to your father for me, James?"

James Jenkins slowly put just the tip of an index finger on the fold of the paper. Then he moved his eyes about one-tenth of an inch and looked at me.

"Okay," he said.

Then James Jenkins, without moving his head or eyes, picked up my entry form and slid it into his pocket, very slowly, like a murderer.

TRAPPED INSIDE THE CAVERN OF DOOM

We start off by getting in trouble, and things get worse and worse from that point on.

Coach Bovard had it in for me, just like James Jenkins told me on day one of eighth grade Boys' PE.

It happened when James Jenkins and I were getting into our (excuse me) stupid Dick Dowling Middle School Mustangs official Boys' PE uniforms. It was raining hard that day, and the fields and track were sloppy with mud, so Coach Bovard's instructions—which were always written on a small whiteboard outside the double-door entry to the boys' locker room—said this:

Dress

Report to Gym

Dodgeball

NO TALKING IN THE LOCKER ROOM!!!

And I was dying to know if he'd given my entry form to his father, but I just couldn't get myself to speak to James Jenkins.

It was Friday, and I had waited two full days for some sign that my entry form had made it into Kenny Jenkins's crooked hands, but as yet there was no indication of that from James. Maybe he read my mind or something. I always thought that murderers were good at stuff like mind reading, anyway.

James Jenkins said, "By the way, I gave your entry form to my father."

At first it kind of scared me that James Jenkins said something to me. To be honest, it looked like he was talking to his locker, because as usual James Jenkins did not move his head. He just sat there on the bench as he took off his shirt, very slowly, and stared directly ahead at the smelly PE stuff in his locker.

It also bothered me that James said "By the way." It was almost as though in his mind he had pressed pause on whatever conversation we may have had in Science Club/Detention two days before.

And it was especially creepy because nobody ever talked at all in the locker room, not since the very first day of dress-out class when I got the entire class punished by telling James Jenkins about (excuse me) stupid camping with my dad. So the locker room always sounded like some kind of automated factory—a soulless machine where no ideas were ever shared openly; just a bunch of clicks and snaps and zippers and locker doors slamming shut and footsteps and (excuse me) flushing toilets and sighs of despair.

That's what the locker room *always* sounded like.

Unless someone talked.

Because if anybody ever talked in the locker room, it was like dropping a bomb in a library, and you were bound to get caught by Coach Bovard, who never *wasn't* watching us.

So when I told James Jenkins "Thank you," Coach Bovard exploded into an angry, steaming hot geyser of rage. He screamed so loud, every boy in the locker room could feel the shock waves rippling through the wet concrete floor and vibrating the rivets and hinges of the rows of metal lockers.

All across Texas, birds fell dead from the sky.

"What are you doing? What do you think you are DOING?" Coach Bovard howled.

In English class, Mrs. Chen had taught us about *rhetorical devices*, which is what I believed Coach Bovard was utilizing in his question, since he quite obviously did not want me or James Jenkins to actually answer him. Because what I was doing and what I *thought* I was doing were the same thing: I was sitting there, frozen in fear, reaching into my (excuse me) dumb locker for my (excuse me) stupid PE T-shirt.

Like a striking rattlesnake, Coach Bovard snatched me by my left arm and James Jenkins by his right arm and marched us toward the CAVERN OF DOOM, which was the small, windowless coach's office next to the showers at the far end of the locker room.

No boy had EVER been inside Coach Bovard's office. We

ANDREW SMITH

only knew it was there, kind of like you know a volcano is there—a sleeping one that can destroy civilization and everything you ever believed was real at any moment. All any of us knew was this was the door in front of which Coach Bovard would stand and watch us like a guard dog on a prison gang, to make sure there was no "horseplay" in the showers.

Why do horses always get blamed for the kind of playing that is not allowed?

Did I mention Coach Bovard's office was windowless? Because that was the worst ingredient in the recipe.

At first I was shocked by the clutter and mess inside Coach Bovard's office. For someone who always seemed so neat and in control of things, Coach Bovard apparently did not enforce standards on his office decor. There were papers and candy wrappers on the floor, the trash can was overflowing, you couldn't even see where the keyboard for his computer was buried, and there were at least four used plastic water bottles (the kind that Karim wanted to build a papyrus reed boat out of) sitting on his desk, and each one of them was partially filled with tobacco spit (these spit bottles are things that everyone in Texas is familiar with—there are so many of them littering our roadsides, they could be mistaken for the official state bird or something).

There was one chair in front of Coach Bovard's desk, and a plastic milk crate that had some file folders on top of it. Coach Bovard swiped the folders onto the messy floor and made me sit down on the milk crate. Then he sat James Jenkins down on the chair and told us (definitely the way a murderer would tell you) not to even think about moving, because he was coming back for us in just a minute.

Neither of us had finished dressing. James Jenkins hadn't even started dressing, to be honest. He was only in his underwear. At least I had gotten into my PE shorts before we were apprehended by Coach Bovard, but we were both barefoot, and neither one of us even had our T-shirt on.

Then Coach Bovard slammed his door shut and left us there, alone in his tiny office.

And from outside, in the dead silence of the locker room, James Jenkins and I heard the jangling of Coach Bovard's keys, the turning of the dead bolt.

Coach Bovard locked James Jenkins and me inside his office.

The office with no windows and no way out.

Then came absolute quiet, followed by pounding thick pulses of blood that seemed to balloon—louder and louder and louder—inside the veins in my tightening neck.

ANDREW SMITH

THE
SECOND
DAY
IN
THE
HOLE

THE ITSY BITSY FOUR-YEAR-OLD

My second day in the hole starts with staring up at a small blob of blue Texas sky.

In the daylight, the opening above me was shaped like a football, or maybe a soft-shell crab, cut from the morning sky. Thinking about soft-shell crab made me hungry. It felt like I'd never *not* been out of the (excuse me) stupid well. And it felt like I would never—*never*—be able to leave it.

The grinding and clanking of machinery tearing through the ground above me shook and rattled everything in the abandoned well, just like how you can feel the weight and power of an arriving train when you're standing on the platform at a station. I did not like it. It frightened me to think that everything around me could collapse in on itself, and I'd be buried alive.

That feeling, claustrophobia, would keep coming back to me as I got older—over and over—much worse sometimes than at others. It was more troubling than sadness and fear and loneliness all rolled together and multiplied by ten thousand. The fear took my breath away; it made me forget all about things like oxygen and inhaling and being somewhere safe.

And there was nothing I could do to make it go away.

Later on, before I started talking again, and before I could go to school with the other kids, Mom and Dad took me to see a therapist, and I even went to a summer camp too. The camp was just for kids like me who needed to work on retraining their brains so we could find a way to stop thinking about the bad things that had happened to us. But the claustrophobia was something that never entirely left once it had wrapped its arms around me and wouldn't let me go.

It was terrible.

And Bartleby, who had already used the excuse that he didn't like being around crowds of noisy people, was gone again. I was alone. I thought maybe Bartleby was still back in Ethan Pixler's secret hideout, talking to the chorus of bats.

Nothing seemed real—like a dream or something—because I couldn't honestly tell the difference between times that I may have been asleep and times when I was awake and listening to the sound of what was going on in the real world up above me.

The real world was just a small blob of crab-shaped sky.

Asleep/Awake/Day/Night/Up/Down—none of it made any difference at all here at the bottom of my abandoned well.

This was the true opposite of the world.

"How's it going, bud?" My dad's voice crackled through the little speaker on the cable.

"Dad? I'm thirsty, Dad. And hungry," I said.

Mom tried to say something to me, but her voice was shaky and strangled from crying. It made me feel awful, because all of this was my fault.

I ruined their lives.

Dad said, "We're going to try to get something down to you. We're working on it right now. And do you hear the digging? The digger crew says we're almost halfway there, Sam! Almost halfway! We'll have you out before you know it."

I thought about what my father was telling me. "Before I knew it" was already gone, and "almost halfway there" meant that Bartleby was right—I would have to end up staying in this well for at least another entire day.

"You should see all the people up here rooting for you, Sam," Dad said.

And he was right. By midmorning of my second day in the well—the day after Thanksgiving—thousands of people had flocked to Blue Creek. Most of them came as spectators, but some were determined to serve as volunteers, hoping to participate in the rescue of the Little Boy in the Well.

By lunchtime (and I still hadn't eaten or had anything to drink), the crowds outside the opening to the well had become a sort of uniformed army, awash in patriotic red-white-and-blue Lone Star Texas T-shirts that said PRAY FOR SAM across their chests. The well-digging crew had been replaced by a utility-company truck called a rathole digger, which was used to plant telephone poles alongside highways.

There were TV cameras and reporters from newspapers and magazines. Blue Creek had never been so famous, and it was all because of me.

It was terrible.

Someone from Blue Creek began scooping up small plastic bags filled with some of the dirt pulled up by the rathole digger. There were plenty of people all over America—and in other places too—who were willing to pay money for bags of dirt from the Little Boy in the Well.

Someone had put up a makeshift flagpole. The United States and Texas flags flew above me and my hole. Over a public address system, the governor of Texas led all the gathered spectators in prayer.

And throughout the day I waited and watched the blue blob above me as it changed colors in the dusty afternoon, and then went gray with clouds once again. They put the tent back up over the mouth of the well, concerned that the rain would return, and my little blob of sky disappeared.

Mom spoke to me in the afternoon. She asked me to tell her something. I didn't really know what to say, so I just asked, "Is it going to be much longer, Mom?"

"It won't be long, honey," Mom said. "Can you sing something for us? Everyone would love to hear you sing, Sam. How about 'Itsy Bitsy Spider'?"

I didn't say anything. I just sat there in my mud and stared at the light coming from the end of the cable—the same place

ANDREW SMITH

where my mom's voice was coming from. "Itsy Bitsy Spider" had to be the worst possible song Mom could ask me to sing—all that stuff about being tiny, and crawling up a hole and getting washed back down.

It was terrifying to think about now.

What was Mom *thinking*?

I listened to the grinding and chewing of the dirt beside the well from the twisting point of the rathole digger.

I said, "I don't really like that song, Mom."

Mom said, "It's okay, honey. You don't have to."

"Sorry, Mom," I said.

Then Mom said, "How about 'Deep in the Heart of Texas'?"

It was not a time when I felt like singing—not even Great-Grandma's song about bloody flowers, or "Deep in the Heart of Texas," which probably was my favorite song, on account of the clapping and stuff. I started to cry again, but this time I didn't make any sound at all. Mom couldn't hear me over the noise of the excavation anyway, but I still didn't want her to feel bad because of my (excuse me) stupidity.

It was awful what I'd done to Mom and Dad, to everyone in Blue Creek, where I already knew I would never again be able to be just another regular kid.

I was so angry at myself for what I'd done, and how I'd ended up all alone down here.

WHAT ARMADILLOS DO FOR FUN

"I start my day slow," Bartleby explained.

Bartleby scratched at the curls of whiskers beneath his chin and added, "Besides, in case you didn't know it, I'm *nocturnal*."

And when Bartleby said "nocturnal," he hooked his dirty claws into air quotes and widened his glossy black eyes. But he was back, and as far as I could tell it was nighttime. The light from the end of the cable was still shining down into the well, and above me the little hole that was shaped like a football or a soft-shell crab was awash in the white-hot glare of spotlights.

The machines continued their digging and digging.

How much longer could it possibly take for all those powerful machines to get as far down as I'd fallen in just about three seconds?

And the day had seemed so long. Above, my rescuers had given up on trying to get food or water down to me. Nothing they tried worked, and they were afraid that they'd block the narrowest parts of the well by attempting to lower food and water containers down there, especially since the camera and light cable had been stuck since the first day. Dad told me that everything would be just fine anyway, and that I'd be out of the well before I really needed anything. Dad's reassurance only ended up making me feel hungrier and thirstier, to the point where I felt like I was about to give up.

But they didn't like it when I stopped talking to them. I was so tired. Someone with a very scary-sounding voice from the Blue Creek Fire Department told me it was critical that I attempt to remain alert and awake so I could talk to the people up above me as much as possible, but I just didn't want to anymore.

And nobody was talking on the outside now anyway. Once again, things had quieted down at night as all the vigilant spectators had gone home or retired into small tents and sleeping bags to wait for any real signs of progress. Everywhere in the field around the mouth of the well, Blue Creek had transformed into a sort of outdoor-festival tent city, but I didn't feel festive at all. Television crews had trailers to live in and work from. During the daytime, I could smell barbecues and hear the sounds of acoustic guitars being played, and people singing songs. People had been enjoying themselves while they waited for the Little Boy in the Well to be either saved or lost.

But Bartleby talked and talked. And the same as I'd done with the voices that had been transmitting through the rescue cable during the day, I just kind of shut him out without really paying attention to anything he was saying, which frustrated Bartleby, who thrived on audience.

Bartleby sighed in exasperation. He grumbled, "Well, if you're just going to lie there staring up at nothing, I may as well go. It *is* Friday night, you know. It's not like I don't already have dozens of other things I could be doing. For *fun*, I mean."

And when Bartleby said "fun," he kind of gyrated his slender armadillo shoulders like he was dancing or something.

"Oh. Sure. Right," I said.

Bartleby never *wasn't* lying.

(Excuse me.) "Darn right I'm right," Bartleby said.

"Okay. So what *do* armadillos do for fun on Friday nights?" I asked.

Bartleby's eyes widened. He said, "Show-and-tell."

"You do show-and-tell? We do that in preschool."

"No, no, no," Bartleby said. He waved a claw back and forth in the air between us like he was erasing the misinformation I'd just delivered to him. "I'll *show* you what I do, and you can *tell* me that you think it's fun."

"Or not," I added.

"You. Are. So. NEGATIVE!" Bartleby said.

But I pointed out, "One of the first things you did to me was—excuse me—poop on my foot. That kind of got us off to a bad start, as far as trust is concerned."

Bartleby laughed. "Ha ha! That was so long ago! You need to get over it, Sam. Move on. Today's the only day we have, and there's never been anything wrong with that! So, two big lessons for you: First, you can't spend your entire life simply trying to avoid disappointing people and *not* falling into holes. And second, you have to learn to let go of things. Those right there are some pretty big truths, Sam. Now, if you're ready to go have some Friday-night fun, possibly meet the Armadillo of Thanksgiving Future, or both—ha ha!—follow me!"

Then Bartleby turned his armadillo chin downward so his body became a ball, and he flipped around and ducked into his tunnel, calling back to me, "Come on, Sam. It's Friday night!"

I could imagine Bartleby's eyes widening and his claws miming a slow-motion fireworks explosion in front of his face when he said "Friday night."

The first time I'd followed Bartleby (and it seemed like it was *months ago*), his tunnel split into three branches. Down the first one we had come to Ethan Pixler's coffin. The second tunnel led us to Ethan Pixler's secret bank robber's hiding place, around fifty-seven cents in pennies and nickels, a bunch of buttons, and about ten thousand bats who all said exactly the same thing at exactly the same time.

We were now in the third tunnel, and I was crawling on my knees, following Bartleby as fast as I could through the dark and dirt.

EIGHTH
GRADE

THE FIRST ENORMOUS TRUTH

I'm going to start by saying it is NOT my fault that I ended up in after-school detention with James Jenkins.

And allow me to also add a bit here about what it is like to have claustrophobia as bad as I do.

Having claustrophobia feels like this: When it hits you, you are more certain that you are going to die than you would be if you were actually in the process of dying.

My claustrophobia was like a next-door neighbor who never spoke to me—one whose name I never knew but who was always right there, waiting to come over, move in, and make himself at home. It had always been difficult for me to understand, because it wasn't until I was quite a bit older that I was able to remember anything at all about being inside the well. That entire time span—three days—is like an erased spot in my life, something I was *told* happened to me, but it was like deep down I didn't really know whether I believed it or not.

Up until the day that James Jenkins and I got locked inside Coach Bovard's windowless, escape-proof office, I had never had an attack of claustrophobia at school. For one thing, my elementary school teachers had all been given lengthy lists of instructions for what to do with the Little Boy in the Well if he started showing signs of a panic attack. But then I got to middle school, and within a week I had been moved from grade six to grade eight. And although my new eighth-grade teachers at Dick Dowling Middle School knew all about Sam Abernathy and the abandoned well (because there was not a soul in Blue Creek who didn't know more about it than I did), I think most of them assumed I was just like any other kid (albeit a very small one, comparatively speaking).

I have always believed that teachers see a formless mass of consciousness when they look at their students, anyway—so why would any of us kids ever need special treatment under any circumstances? This was middle school, after all, the place where kids need to figure it out on their own, learn how to manage setbacks and be tough, and just *grow up*.

So it was pretty much as soon as Coach Bovard locked me and James Jenkins inside the impenetrable CAVERN OF DOOM that my heart began to race. Hearing the dead bolt slide into place, I could no longer catch my breath, and my vision began to go dark around the edges.

I can't remember too much after that, because the next thing I knew I was lying curled up on my side on the floor of Coach Bovard's messy office, and at that moment James Jenkins the murderer, who for reasons I could not understand was only in his underwear, was holding up my head, trying to roll me onto my back. And James Jenkins was looking directly into my eyes, asking me if I was okay, while Coach Bovard screamed at us for (excuse me) *screwing around* in his (excuse me) *damn* office.

Then, after he calmed down a bit and stopped shaking, Coach Bovard ordered me and James to go directly to the principal's office, without even letting us get dressed back into our school clothes. At least he allowed us to put on T-shirts, and he let James get into his PE shorts. There are strict rules at Dick Dowling Middle School about walking around campus in your underwear and with no shirt on, after all.

But that's how I ended up in after-school detention with James Jenkins.

I had never gotten in trouble at school in my life.

It was like falling into a well all over.

Once again, I was sure that I'd ruined Mom's and Dad's (and now my little brother's and sister's) lives for good.

At least it wasn't Science Club day, so I was spared the humiliation of serving detention in front of Karim and Bahar, or Michael Dolgoff, the worm farm kid who wanted to make bugs fight in an arena. But James Jenkins and I had to spend the last two hours of the school day in the principal's office in our PE clothes while all kinds of grown-ups and kids we didn't know looked at us, and then sat for an additional hour after school in our homeroom—Mr. Mannweiler's classroom—while

Mr. Mannweiler pretended to pay attention to us, although he was obviously reading a magazine about basketball.

James Jenkins and I were also both given half sheets of photocopied instructions. The papers told us we had to write a full two-page essay on what rules we broke, why we felt motivated to break them, and what our plan of action (our P.O.A., as Dad would say) would be, in order to not ever break those rules in the future.

I raised my hand to get Mr. Mannweiler's attention, but he was too engrossed in his basketball magazine, so I kept my arm up until it hurt. Finally, Mr. Mannweiler noticed. He sighed and looked at me without saying anything, which was enough to tell me that he didn't want to be bothered by me.

I said, "Mr. Mannweiler, do you have a thesaurus I could use?"

Mr. Mannweiler looked at James Jenkins. Then he looked at the bookcase where all the science textbooks were stacked.

Mr. Mannweiler sighed. He said, "Use easy words, Abernathy. It's detention. There's no Pulitzer Prize in detention."

I guessed that meant *no*.

James didn't even look at his instructions. He obviously didn't need to. He went right to work on his essay while I toiled over crafting a captivating opening paragraph. In fact, it was with a reasonable amount of jealousy and doubt that I viewed James Jenkins when he finished his full two-page essay in less than twenty minutes.

I was still on page one.

I figured that, unlike with other things they do, murderers must write fast, and that they're probably not concerned about neatness, spelling, or grammar. But, without moving his head, James Jenkins straightened up in the desk right next to me, brushed the eraser crumbs away from his paper using the blade of his right hand, then slowly stood and walked across the room to Mr. Mannweiler's desk.

James Jenkins dropped his essay into the wire basket with a sign on it that said IN.

Mr. Mannweiler didn't say anything. He just glanced at the clock.

We had forty minutes to go.

James Jenkins turned around without moving his head or saying anything to Mr. Mannweiler. Then—like a murderer— he walked very slowly toward me and sat down once again at his desk.

I figured by this point James Jenkins probably had a memorized formula for his after-school-detention essays. He probably only had to change key terms like "murdering a kid at recess" to "talking while in my underwear."

"How did you do that so fast?" I whispered.

Let me explain that I normally would not have said anything to James Jenkins, but ever since Coach Bovard screamed at us in his office I found myself wondering why it could have been that James Jenkins would have apparently been trying to help me—as opposed to trying to murder me, which is probably what he would have done if Coach Bovard had not returned when he did.

James Jenkins had his hands flat on the top of his desk. He moved his eyes (but not his chin) about one-tenth of an inch in my direction, and, facing toward the front of Mr. Mannweiler's classroom, James Jenkins said this: "I like to write."

This was information I was unprepared to deal with.

James Jenkins had flunked eighth grade. He couldn't *possibly* like to write. He had to have been messing with me. Maybe I was still a bit out of it after what happened in Coach Bovard's office. Maybe James Jenkins really only liked to write ransom notes, or instructions about where bodies were hidden, or cheerful little reminders to people telling them joyful things like *You're next*.

I think James Jenkins must have noticed (out of the tiniest corner of his unmoving eye) that I was staring at him in a kind of puzzled disbelief, because with no prompting from me at all he added, "I like to read, too."

Then James Jenkins said this: "What's your favorite book?"

This really put me on the spot. I never for a moment would have guessed James Jenkins would have asked me a question about books. I was so confused. Maybe it was something that murderers do—confusing their victims, I mean—kind of like what cobras do, or something.

I actually touched the side of my head to reassure myself it had not exploded.

"I. Uh." I couldn't even think. "*Dune. Dune* is my favorite book," I gasped.

I was so completely confused.

James Jenkins nodded. It wasn't a real nod; it was the kind of nod a murderer who appreciated science fiction would do, which is to say he moved his chin downward about one-thirtieth of an inch.

"*Dune* is awesome. One of my favorites for sure," James Jenkins said. He looked directly ahead. He did not move.

I glanced over at Mr. Mannweiler. He had no clue James Jenkins and I were talking. About writing. And books.

But an eighth-grade student who reads a book as heavy as *Dune* couldn't possibly flunk out of school, right? James Jenkins *had* to be messing with me. I considered asking him the timelessly effective question *What was your favorite part of Dune, James Jenkins—MURDERER?* but then I realized that might be a really good way to get myself killed, so instead I said, "But you flunked eighth grade."

Which, as soon as the words left my mouth, I thought they would probably get me killed too.

"I didn't flunk," James Jenkins said. "I was *held back*."

I didn't understand. I always thought being *held back* was the nice way of not having to admit you *flunked*. Because, after all, you get *held back* when you can't pass your classes, which equals flunking, right?

Then, almost as though he felt the need to clarify the

matter, James Jenkins added, "My father thought it would be a good thing for me if he held me back one year."

James Jenkins could not possibly be more of my opposite than he was, I thought.

And I desperately wanted to ask him why his father thought it would be good for him, but I couldn't get the words out of my throat. It struck me that being held back a year because your father thought it was good for you had to be just as awful as being skipped ahead—maybe even worse than being skipped ahead—but it was something that I never thought about until James Jenkins told me that. Another thing I hadn't really thought about was my essay, because all of a sudden Mr. Mannweiler flipped his basketball magazine shut and said, "I'm letting you guys go fifteen minutes early so you can get dressed. Get out of here. I need to go take a dump."

(Excuse me.)

James Jenkins got up faster than I'd ever seen him move, which was still really slow. I guess freedom has that effect on murderers and essayists. And although I wasn't finished with my essay, I decided to bring it to a quick close, so I wrote THE END halfway down the middle of page two. I rationalized that you don't get grades for detention, so it probably didn't matter that my essay was terrible.

Like Mr. Mannweiler said: There are no Pulitzer Prizes in after-school detention.

So I flipped my paper into Mr. Mannweiler's IN basket

and left detention, hopefully for the last time in my life.

James Jenkins was outside in the empty hallway, spinning the ticking tumbler very slowly—*click . . . click . . . click!*—for the combination on his locker, which happened to be right next to mine. Naturally, he didn't look at me as I opened my locker.

It was still raining outside, and I needed my coat for the walk home. I already knew I'd be in trouble if Mom found out why I was so late. Maybe I could hang out at Karim's for a while, I thought—practice a macaroni and cheese recipe or something. Dad would still be at Lily Putt's, which never shut down because of weather, on account of the fact that we had an entire second course that was indoors.

But I needed to know more about James Jenkins's story. There was something about the kid who nearly murdered me during a game of Spud seven years ago that didn't make sense. The James Jenkins I had long imagined was not holding up to the James Jenkins who tried to help me in Coach Bovard's office—or the James Jenkins who spoke to me in complete sentences about writing, and about reading books.

James grabbed a backpack and his coat from his locker, slammed the locker door shut, and started walking away from me—down the deserted hallway and toward the boys' locker room. The stiff rubber soles of James Jenkins's Converse sneakers tap-tapped like the drumbeat accompaniment to a condemned man's walk to the gallows.

I grabbed my coat and followed him.

I swallowed hard and thought about the meaningless content of my great-grandmother's song "I Will Walk with Him in the Garden of Blood," which is something I usually thought about when I also thought I was about to be murdered. I especially thought about it now that I was walking with James Jenkins in the empty hallway of linoleum at Dick Dowling Middle School, on our way to the very creepy and empty boys' locker room.

I said, "Um. James. I forgot to tell you thanks for trying to look out for me today in Coach Bovard's office."

James didn't react beyond saying something with his mouth closed. It sounded like, "Hmft."

So I added, "I get claustrophobia really bad sometimes."

James Jenkins stopped moving. It was like he was having a stare-down contest with the sign that said PUSH on the door to the locker room. After about twenty seconds—when the stare-down with the sign had apparently ended in a draw—James Jenkins pivoted his entire upper body (but not his chin), so he was looking directly at me (which made me think he was about to murder me), and said, "I bet you do. It must be really awful."

James Jenkins leaned his upper arm into the locker room door and slowly eased it open.

I said, "Yeah. I do. And it is. So, thanks. Um. Thank you. James. Jenkins."

James Jenkins shrugged, which is to say he raised both of

his shoulders approximately one-sixtieth of an inch. He said, "No problem, Well Boy. Blow-vard hates you anyway. And I thought you stopped breathing, besides."

I inhaled, just to make sure my air bags still worked. Then, with some degree of disgust, I said, "Oh. Would you have done mouth-to-mouth resuscitation on me?"

I was horrified.

James Jenkins said, "Well. I do know how to do it, if I have to. I took a course."

I nodded—a normal, non-murderer nod, one where your chin actually goes up and down.

I'll admit it: I didn't really want to be alone in an empty locker room with James Jenkins, who would have done mouth-to-mouth resuscitation on me (probably only to revive me enough so he could murder me), but there was no way I was going to walk all the way back home in my PE uniform either. I thought about just putting my coat on and going to Karim's and borrowing clothes from him, but when you're in eighth grade, coming home from school wearing a different outfit than you left home in is not a workable plan. That would mean trouble for sure.

Having nobody in there with us made the locker room seem even more creepy and dungeonlike than if Coach Bovard were breathing down our necks and making sure there was no talking or gum chewing. Half the lights were turned off, and there was a steady and menacing *drip, drip, drip* coming from inside the showers. It was the kind of scene no one would be surprised to see in a movie about a murderer.

I sat down on the bench next to James Jenkins, slipped off my tennis shoes, and opened my gym locker. I started pulling out my school clothes, listening to the dripping sounds that echoed in the concrete cavern.

Grateful to still be alive, I slipped my arms into my school shirt and said, "Well, I'm just curious, but why did your dad think holding you back in eighth grade would be a good idea? I didn't think anyone ever got . . . um . . . *held back* in middle school."

And that was when I found out the first enormous truth about James Jenkins.

Because James Jenkins told me this: "My father did it for football."

I didn't understand. I thought everyone in Blue Creek believed James Jenkins was going to be a star in football, so why would Kenny Jenkins keep his son from going to high school, where he could be the star of the team everyone in our little town worshipped as some sort of hundred-legged, fifty-headed god?

"But I thought he wanted you to play football for Blue Creek."

James Jenkins was tying his shoelaces. Slowly. He didn't move his chin. It was almost as though he were talking to his foot. He nodded. Well, I *thought* James Jenkins nodded. The movement was so slight, it may have been just the pulse in his neck. I couldn't be sure. James said, "He does. And he wants me to be one year bigger than any other high school quarterback in the state. It's the plan for getting me into the University of Texas and playing for the Longhorns. That's why he held me back. So I could grow."

That sounded like some kind of science experiment from a horror film.

I finished getting dressed, trying to calculate whether or not I had ever heard anything dumber or more unfair in my life than holding your own kid back—making him *flunk*—just so he could grow twelve months bigger than other kids who wanted to play a (excuse me) stupid game.

I hadn't.

I said, "Oh my gosh. Excuse me. That sucks."

James Jenkins continued to talk to his shoe. He said, "Yeah. It doesn't matter. I hate football, anyway."

My head spun. This was all too much, trying to deal with a new reality in which James Jenkins enjoyed writing, actually read books, and *hated football*.

"You do?" I said.

I had known James Jenkins pretty much all my life. While it was true that I'd never really talked to him after he caused me to fall down the well when I was four years old, I at least *thought* I knew who James Jenkins was. The James Jenkins I *thought* I knew was in many ways the collective beliefs of everyone who lived in Blue Creek. And the collective beliefs of an entire town had to be right, right? This kid tying his shoes next to me in the locker room at Dick Dowling Middle School was *not* the James Jenkins I had nightmares about.

"I can't stand football. I hate everything about it. I hate watching it on TV. I hate seeing guys paint longhorns on their bellies. I hate Gatorade, especially the green kind. I hate thinking that I can't do what I want to do," James Jenkins said. "My father *forces* me to play."

I was suddenly very sad, for so many reasons that all jumbled up in my head.

Then James Jenkins said, "You know what, though? When I go to stay with my mom during summers and at Christmas, she signs me up for dance class."

James Jenkins's mother lived in Austin.

I nearly passed out. Maybe James Jenkins and I had accidentally slipped into another dimension or something. Maybe Coach Bovard's office was the portal to an alternate universe. That had to have been the explanation.

James Jenkins and I broke the universe.

"You . . . um . . . *dance*?" I asked.

"I love to dance," James said, watching the door of his locker as he snapped it shut. "My dad won't let me do it here. There's not enough time, due to football season, he says. And in Blue Creek, football season never ends. I hate football."

Then James Jenkins stood up, very slowly.

Without looking at me, he said, "Do you have to walk home? I'll go with you."

I felt dizzy.

I said, "I don't have an umbrella."

James Jenkins may have shrugged, possibly, and said, "Neither do I."

IN WHICH WE BREAK THE UNIVERSE

It starts by me telling the story of my after-school deten- tion over macaroni and cheese with Karim and Bahar.

Another week had ended at Dick Dowling Middle School.

And another weekend arrived when Dad and I would be abandoned somewhere in the Texas wilderness for survival camping—rain or shine, as Dad liked to forebode.

"Supposedly, James Jenkins has read *Dune*. He said it was 'awesome,'" I said.

And when I said "awesome," I hooked my fingers into air quotes and made my eyes into big circles, which kind of gave me a feeling of déjà vu, but I had no idea where it came from.

Strange.

Bahar nodded and gave me a suspicious look. Of course, she'd read every *Dune* book there was, including the ones that weren't written by Frank Herbert.

Bahar said, "You should have given him the idiot test. You know, ask him what his favorite part of the book was."

I shook my head. "I thought about doing that. But then I

realized that if he really *did* read it, he might kill me for doubting him; and if he *didn't* read it, he might kill me for trying to trap him. Either way it wasn't going to end well."

Karim scraped his spoon noisily across his plate. He said, "Giving the benefit of the doubt is a good way to avoid a surprise encounter with natural selection. And this is prize-winning mac and cheese, Sam."

My clothes tumbled around inside the dryer while we ate. Karim ended up loaning me some pajamas and a robe while I waited for them to finish drying. By the time I'd gotten to Karim's house, I looked like I was a shipwreck victim, plucked from the middle of the ocean. So did James Jenkins when we got to his house, which was across the clearing in the woods where the now-sealed "Sam's Well" was located, a good half mile closer to school than my house was.

I didn't confess to Karim and Bahar that James Jenkins and I actually walked home from school *together*. It may have been too much for them to take. I didn't even know if I believed it, because James Jenkins was all of a sudden no longer James Jenkins, and I didn't know how I felt about that.

On the way, two different cars pulled up alongside us and the drivers asked James if he wanted a ride. James Jenkins was a guaranteed future football hero in Blue Creek, and everyone was counting on that. And James told both of the drivers no thanks, but each one of them also said something along the lines of "Hey! Isn't that the kid who fell in the well?"

James Jenkins, in his usual murderous style, said nothing, just kept his eyes forward and continued walking next to me—slowly, which made us both much wetter than we would have been if we had walked at a non-murderer-in-a-rainstorm pace, or especially if we had accepted a ride from a creepy football-loving stranger.

In fact, when we got to James Jenkins's house, he told me that nobody was home—that nobody was ever home, because his father was always at Colonel Jenkins's Diner. Then James Jenkins asked me if I wanted to come inside and use a towel, or borrow something dry to put on, or have some hot chocolate or something.

I stood there at his front door, dripping. I shook my head and said, "I still have a ways to go anyway, but thanks for offering. Um . . . James."

Maybe James Jenkins was actually trying to be nice to me, and not merely attempting to lure me inside his HOUSE OF DEATH so he could murder me behind closed doors, where nobody would see—not that any likely witnesses were out and about in this wooded and empty end of Blue Creek, on account of the storm.

"Yeah. Well, no worries, Sam," James said. It struck me that James Jenkins had never once in the past seven years called me Sam. To him, I had always been Well Boy, just like I had always been to all the other people in Blue Creek.

I stood there for a long, quiet minute, dripping.

ANDREW SMITH

It was a very awkward good-bye.

"Well. I'll . . . uh . . . see you in Mannweiler's Monday," I said.

"You want to come over or something this weekend?" James Jenkins said.

I was right—we *did* break the universe.

"I can't. I'm going camping with my dad tomorrow," I said.

"Oh. Lucky," James said.

"Not the way my dad makes us do it. It's torture. We eat bugs and trash, and I have to sleep outside, on account of my . . . uh . . . *thing*."

"Claustrophobia?"

"Yeah."

"Even if it rains?"

"Even if it rains," I affirmed.

"Oh," James Jenkins said. He stared directly ahead at the little beveled glass windows in his front door.

I slosh-turned to leave.

"Hey, hang on a second," James said. "I want to show you something."

Then James Jenkins squeezed his hand inside the soggy front pocket of his jeans and started to pull something out. This was it, I thought. This was the classic moment in all murder movies when the secret and deadly weapon is pulled on the unsuspecting victim.

Surprise!

As I stood there, I braced myself for the impact of the universe coming back together as James Jenkins the kind-of-nice, kind-of-sad guy I got in trouble with and walked home from school with transformed back into James Jenkins the murderer. Then James pulled out his cell phone, which, like everything else in this small part of the torn-asunder universe, was wet. He pulled up his shirttail and wiped the screen of his phone dry on his undershirt, then began entering something into it.

James Jenkins held his phone in front of me so I could see what he'd brought up on the screen.

The screen showed a website for a place called Acceleration, which was obviously a dance school—the one in Austin that James Jenkins had told me about.

There were two noticeable photos of James Jenkins on the school's home page, like he was the star of the school or something. And I'll be perfectly honest—I had never really *looked* at James Jenkins in this way before. How could I? But seeing those pictures of him, the confident expression on his face, how alive his eyes looked, and how much he seemed to fit in with what he was doing, well, if I owned a dance school (which I never would do) and I wanted people to think I ran a *good* dance school, I would use pictures just like the ones Acceleration posted of James Jenkins to show people what a great place it was.

In one of the pictures James stood beside a white horizontal rail (called a barre, he told me), holding on to it with one hand. In the photo, James Jenkins was wearing gray tights (that were so tight they made him look [excuse me] naked) and a white undershirt with a neckline that opened all the way down his chest. James held up one leg extended behind him, with his toes pointing higher than his head, while he reached out his other arm straight from his shoulder, fingers bent inward slightly, his eyes focused directly on his hand, with an expression on his face that looked so calm and proud and radiant. There was a little sweat around his hairline and on his neck.

Below the picture of James Jenkins at the barre was a link: BREAKING THE BARRIERS: AUSTIN'S BALLET BOY WONDER.

In the other image James was dressed in baggy jeans, a tank top, and loose Adidas sneakers, and he was upside down, with just one hand on the floor supporting himself like the trunk of an improbable tree, legs toward the sky, knees bent, both feet kicking out in opposite directions, his free hand seeming to casually rest flat on the sole of one of his shoes. And again, the expression on his face projected a kind of attitude that he could do this all day long—and that he loved doing it too.

James Jenkins pointed at the picture of him at the barre. "This one's taken in contemporary dance class. It's actually Russian ballet. It's crazy hard, but it's my favorite. You have to wear tights, and you pick up your partners sometimes and lift them over your head."

"Did you ever drop one?" I asked.

James Jenkins laughed. Well, it wasn't actually a *laugh*, because it was still James Jenkins, after all (I think). He smiled, which is to say the edges of his mouth twitched about a seventieth of an inch.

He said, "No."

Then James Jenkins pointed at the other photo—the one where he was upside down in the middle of sticking a one-armed handstand. He said, "This one's hip-hop. It's fun, because when people see you do it they get excited. Everyone gets hip-hop and break dancing. It's different from ballet, which is almost like you need a translator to understand what's going on. That's what I like most about ballet, though, and how it's impossibly hard at times."

"But wait. I saw you at the Back-to-School Dance, and you were just running around. How come you didn't dance there?" I asked.

James Jenkins kind of shrugged, I think. He said, "Nobody ever knew until now. I always think people will laugh, because everyone says I should do football. And I didn't want people to make fun of me."

I looked at the pictures on the phone.

I almost thought about asking *this* James Jenkins what he did with the *other* James Jenkins's body. But then I glanced at James and it was all real. He really *was* the kid in the pictures, I really *did* walk home with him, and we really *did* break the universe that day.

I said, "Wow. That's pretty amazing. Um . . . James. Do boys do dance at the University of Texas?"

James Jenkins shook his head, which was actually only about a fiftieth of an inch in each direction, and said, "Not if they're Kenny Jenkins's kid they don't."

I said, "Yeah. I get it."

But by the time I'd slogged my way through the field behind James Jenkins's house, I had almost convinced myself that nothing that happened to me that day actually happened. I stopped at the site of the old well—"Sam's Well."

Maybe *that* never happened too. I couldn't remember those days anyway, so it was almost as if the broken concrete and rebar that had been piled up over the place where the crews had filled in the opening established some kind of testimony to a false memory. And that false memory included an official yellow sign that said DANGER: UNSTABLE GROUND, on which somebody had scrawled a skull and crossbones and this little caption:

Pray for Sam

But I did not tell my friends Karim and Bahar anything about what James Jenkins and I talked about that day. In many ways I believed that James Jenkins really didn't want people to know about the kid he was not, and the kid he wished he was, and I felt a little strange that, for whatever reasons, after all these years had gone by, James Jenkins had decided to tell *me*, as though I maybe had some power to help him be okay with things.

It was very confusing.

And when Karim complimented the food I'd made for them, I kind of snapped out of the shock and confusion that had been plaguing me ever since PE class.

So I forced my guilty brain (I had no idea *why* I felt guilty, but I did) to change subjects. I said, "Speaking of macaroni and cheese, Karim, you'll never guess what I did."

And I told Karim and Bahar about Kenny Jenkins's (excuse me) dumb macaroni and cheese championship at Blue Creek days, and how I'd entered it, but I was afraid to tell Mom and Dad (probably in the same way that James Jenkins had never shown those pictures of himself dancing to his father either, but I didn't say one word about that to them, because I just didn't know what I was supposed to do about anything anymore.)

I was not good at figuring things out.

THIS IS *NOT* A VEGETARIAN CIRCUS; OR, FILL IN THE BLANK

This starts near the end of a brutally long day, over a meal of actual bugs, with a challenge to my father.

Actual bugs—worms, to be exact.

(Excuse me.)

Michael Dolgoff—the Science Club kid who wanted to make a combat arena for black widows and cicadas or whatever—would probably have been envious, whereas I found myself caught somewhere between disgust and a sudden and intense urge to run away from home and join a circus.

A vegetarian circus.

Survival camping with Dad was rarely fun. I'll be honest: It actually *never* was fun. And now, after spending the last twenty hours without sleep, in on-and-off rain and constant mud, with absolutely nothing on except for some soggy shorts, huddling beneath a rigged "debris canopy" of woven tree limbs while Dad struggled to get a tinder-starved fire started, this particular trip was as not-fun as being locked inside Coach Bovard's CAVERN OF DOOM. And after all the rain of the past two days, finding a supply of "resources" (as Dad calls it—I call it trash) had been particularly difficult. At least the weather had not taken a full turn toward the chill of winter yet.

Fortunately, I talked Dad out of making me wear my Clan Abernathy kilt, which he tried to get me to do for this trip. He wore his, though. So there we were: out in the rain and mud, practically naked, and starving—a barefoot, undersized eleven-year-old boy who dreamed of one day being a world-class chef, dressed only in a pair of shorts, and his father, who looked like he had nothing on but a parochial schoolgirl's skirt.

We might survive the elements and eating garbage, but one of these days some drunk Texan with a gun was going to over-react to the ridiculous image we presented.

It was miserable out there. And it was nearly ten at night by the time Dad finally got a few twigs to smoke and offer up a weak little flame. But we hadn't been so lucky as to find an old hubcap or used beer can this time. Dad unearthed a wad of old aluminum foil from the ashes of a long-abandoned campfire. He carefully unfolded the foil and shaped it into a shallow pan for cooking things. That took about three hours. The rest of our time was consumed by trying to make his debris canopy against the rain, and then Dad trying to start a fire.

We had left home that day earlier than usual, at two in the morning.

"Ah! There she is!" Dad was extremely proud of the fire he'd achieved after being out in the rain for nearly one entire rotation

ANDREW SMITH

of the earth. I was so tired, I could barely keep my eyes open, but I knew better than to plead with him that we should give up and go find a way to call Mom, to have her come rescue us.

Dad went on. "See, Sam? We got this. The key is simply to never quit. You tell yourself what the *one thing* you want most of all is—in this case, fire—and you keep working for that *one thing* until it's yours!"

And when Dad said "one thing," he made air quotes with his fingers.

Weird.

Dad had caught a dozen or so earthworms, which he carried inside a cone he fashioned from a piece of tree bark. He tipped the cone toward the firelight so I could see the things—living, glistening purple spaghetti—and he said, "It's okay to eat these raw in an emergency, Sam, but as a precaution against swallowing any types of parasites, you should always try to cook them first if you can. They taste better that way, besides!"

Everyone knows parasites taste better when you cook them.

And I watched in horror as Dad dumped the blob of living worms into his little dirty tinfoil pan of boiling water. Then he added some wild herbs and stirred his worm soup with a twig.

Dad explained that it took only about two minutes to cook earthworms.

I told him to take as much time as he wanted.

We ate with chopsticks whittled from tree branches. It was the worst thing I had ever had in my mouth—even worse than the gravy that comes with Colonel Jenkins's chicken-fried steak on a stick. The worm soup tasted like pureed dirt, and the worms themselves were salty and had the texture of soft-boiled eggs mixed with warm cottage cheese and glue. I gagged when I swallowed them, and when I did manage to get them down, it felt like most of the gluey parts painted the inside of my mouth and throat and would not go away. But I did it for Dad, and because I wanted him to be in a happy and satisfied frame of mind. I was determined to tell Dad the things that had been building up inside me ever since I started attending Dick Dowling Middle School.

To be honest, they'd been building inside me ever since I got out of the well seven years ago.

Growing up (excuse me) sucks.

"We are very lucky men, Sam," Dad said.

Mrs. Chen, my English teacher, would have been pleased. I could have thought of dozens of adjectives to describe us. *Lucky* did not immediately come to mind. It was past midnight, and the rain began to pick up again.

The worm goo made my tongue stick to the roof of my mouth. I cleared my throat, but it didn't do much good.

I said, "Dad, I need to talk to you about something."

Dad leaned forward and placed a few sticks onto his fire. He had a piece of boiled earthworm and some dirt stuck to the whiskers on his upper lip. And he looked absolutely thrilled.

Dad said, "Is this . . . about *girls*, Sam?"

ANDREW SMITH

And when he said "girls," Dad's eyes got wide and shiny. It reminded me of someone I knew, but I couldn't nail down exactly who it was.

Weird.

Dad scooted closer to me, as though he were expecting me to reveal some deep and telling secret about myself, which I *was* about to do, even if it wasn't anything at all related to the secret about *girls* or whatever Dad had dreamed up in his own head about me.

Maybe that's the key to unlocking everything for kids like me, and for kids like James Jenkins, too: finding some way to erase the limits of the dreams our parents have for our lives. Even if we are just kids, as they see us.

I said, "No, Dad, it is not about girls."

Dad's grin deflated.

He said, "Is it about *boys*?"

His eyes got serious and somber.

My eyes got rolly and upturned.

I almost wished for another mouthful of worms at that point. Why do parents *always* make it impossible to talk to them?

I took a deep breath. My mouth was still sticky.

I said, "Dad? You remember the other day when we went to Colonel Jenkins's—when I went up to the counter and talked to James—Jimmy—Jenkins before we left?"

My dad's eyes became double full moons in the light of our worm bake.

He said, "This is about *Jimmy Jenkins*?"

I looked at my father. His face showed a hint of astonishment mixed with pride and maybe a little shock. His eyes were open, but he wasn't seeing me. He was looking into a future that would never be real.

Why are fathers like that? I mean, it was like all Dad ever did was fill in the blanks for me as though my life were some kind of a test. And if this *was* a test, Dad would get every fill-in wrong. At that point I wasn't ever about to tell him how James Jenkins and I had spent detention together, and then how we walked home and talked about things, and then how it felt almost as though I could actually *become friends* with James Jenkins, because I knew things about James Jenkins that nobody else knew, things nobody else would even believe.

I sighed. "Dad?"

Dad said, "What?"

"Will you let me talk? This is *not* about me and James Jenkins. It's not about me and anybody. Well, it *is* about me and *me*, I guess."

"Oh. Sorry, Son."

I might say that Dad looked embarrassed, but he had worm guts on his face and was out in the rain with nothing on but a (excuse me) stupid kilt, and I don't think anything could ever possibly embarrass him, anyway.

So I continued, "It's okay. But the thing is . . . Well, here's what it is. . . . The thing, I mean."

ANDREW SMITH

It was hard for me to talk to my dad, but then again I was the one who'd put him and Mom through all the trouble after I got trapped in the well seven years ago, so I really didn't want to let them down again. I bit the inside of my cheek. It tasted like worms.

I said, "The thing is, the other day when I talked to James, it was because I want to enter the Blue Creek Days thing."

Dad patted my bare knee. His hand was muddy and wet and cold.

He said, "I know that, Son! We got the permission slip from Mr. Mannweiler for the Science Club display. Extraterrestrial life! That sounds creepy and spectacular!"

My Dad: Perpetual filler-in of all my blanks.

I said, "Dad. No. Here it is, Dad: I don't want to go to MIT. I don't want to have Advanced Placement Physics and go to Blue Creek Magnet School next year. I want to cook, Dad. I want to enter Colonel Jenkins's, excuse me, stupid macaroni and cheese cook-off competition and meet celebrity chef Resa O'Hare, because I know I could win. And I want to get away from Blue Creek, where everybody prays for me and where I'll never not be the, excuse me, dumb Little Boy in the Well. And I want to go to school somewhere that isn't Texas, where there aren't any abandoned wells and where nobody knows who I am—or was—because Resa O'Hare teaches in Oregon at one of the best private high schools in the world for kids who want to learn the culinary arts. Blue Creek Days.

That's what I wanted to tell you, Dad. Are you listening?"

And then I stopped suddenly for two reasons: First, I had let everything spill out so quickly, I wasn't sure exactly what I'd just said to Dad; and second, my stomach was tightening up in convulsions because I was about to start crying.

Either that, or the worms had made a rough landing down there.

Being eleven years old and telling your dad he has everything wrong about you is rough.

The moons of Dad's eyes got noticeably dimmer and smaller. He sat up straight, like he'd been stung by a bee or something. Looking at him made me feel worse, like I'd done something really terrible to my own father, but it was too late to suck all those words back in and let things go on the same as they'd gone for the past seven years.

I'd let my dad down again.

Dad said, "Oh. Hmm . . ."

And that was it.

I said, "Dad?" Then I touched my index finger to the top of my lip and said, "You . . . uh . . . got some . . . uh . . . worm."

Dad wiped at his mouth with the back of his hand and said, "Oh! Heh-heh. Well. I guess we should try to get some shut-eye, Sam. It's been a long day. A really long day."

THE
SECOND
NIGHT
IN
THE
HOLE

A MATTER OF MATHEMATICAL OPTIMISM

It starts underground in the dark, with a bit of math.

Bartleby's third tunnel took me farther away from the well than I'd been on either of our previous trips.

"Too bad none of your tunnels point up," I said. "We could have been out of here days ago."

"Out? OUT? Who wants *out*?" Bartleby asked, his voice slightly muted by the closeness of the dirt walls.

"Well. I do," I said. "You *could* dig . . . um . . . toward *up*, couldn't you?"

Bartleby stopped dead in the middle of the tunnel. My face bumped into his (excuse me) butt.

Bartleby said, "I would prefer not to."

Bartleby pressed forward, and I followed.

Then, as usual, Bartleby continued talking. "Besides, as well as being *nocturnal*, I am also *subterranean*."

"Well, I'm neither one of those things," I said.

"Ha ha! *I'm neither one of those things!*" Bartleby wrenched his voice into a sneering mock of my own. "Well, guess what,

Sam. It's the middle of the night, and you're underground, so I guess you don't even really know *what* you're supposed to be, do you? Subterranean. Plus. Nocturnal."

I stopped following Bartleby. It got very dark.

I realized that all this time I'd been underground with him, whenever Bartleby was around I could see perfectly fine, but once he was away from me, it was impossibly dark.

I said, "You're really mean, Bartleby."

Then I started to back up, feeling my way in reverse toward the well.

Ahead of me in the blackness of the tunnel, Bartleby said, "Hey! What are you doing? Don't be like that. I was only messing around, Sam. Besides, you've GOT to see where I'm taking you."

"I'm tired," I said.

"Oh, kid. You haven't begun to live yet. Look, number one—don't go living your life only trying to avoid holes; number two—the only thing that matters is where you're going, not where you've been; and number three—don't *ever* let anyone tell you that deep down you really aren't a subterranean, nocturnal animal, if that's what you want to be. Because that's what we are!"

Then came the most horrifying noise. It sounded something like a cat with its tail caught in a coffee grinder, if you can imagine what that would sound like. It scared me enough that I jumped, which, because I was on my hands and knees, made me crash my head and shoulders into the roof of Bartleby's tunnel.

"What was that?" I said.

"That? That was my *subterranean nocturnal armadillo roar!*"

And, even though it was pitch-dark, I imagined Bartleby making air quotes and his eyes getting bigger and blacker when he said "subterranean nocturnal armadillo roar."

And Bartleby added, "It's what we *subterranean nocturnal animals do.*"

I did not respond to Bartleby.

"Hey, kid," Bartleby said.

"What?"

"Did I ever show you how I can prove I'm a unicorn? Ha ha!!!"

I groaned and pushed away from Bartleby, continuing to back up.

"Look," Bartleby called after me, "I am just messing around, kid. Lighten up. Besides, I've got a *surprise* for you."

I had been surprised enough. In fact, I was in a constant state of surprise—and I said so to Bartleby.

"This is different," Bartleby countered. "I promise. But if I tell you what it is, it will ruin the surprise. Nobody wants that. So, come on, Sam—embrace your inner subterranean nocturnal animal self! After all, it's your last night down here, so let's have fun."

I inched toward Bartleby. "Wait. Why are you saying it's my last night? What's that supposed to mean?"

I will admit that Bartleby's prediction about this being my last night in the well—or wherever we were—made me feel light and happy, but at the same time I was filled with an ominous sort of dread. What if it was my actual last night *anywhere*?

What if this was it?

Bartleby turned around and scooted back in my direction. He said, "I did the math. They said they were halfway to you yesterday. They've got to be just a matter of hours away from making contact with their Little Boy in the Well. It's a matter of calculation! Ha ha! You can call it *mathematical optimism*."

And when Bartleby said "mathematical optimism," he poked his little wet nose right into mine, widened his inky black eyes, and made air quotes with his sharp and muddy front claws.

I don't know why I trusted Bartleby's mathematical optimism. Maybe it had something to do with my only being four years old at the time. I think the default attitude for most four-year-olds must be optimism, with or without math. That all changes around the time you get into middle school, though, but nobody tells you. But when Bartleby (who never stopped talking anyway) said, "Come on!" I sighed and followed him deeper into the tunnel, resigned to the fact that there was nothing I could do to ever stop Bartleby from manipulating my trust, based on all his math and optimism.

"We're almost there, Sam!" Bartleby said.

"You've been lost before," I pointed out.

"Lost? How can I possibly get lost? This is my world. I made it."

"So I suppose that makes you something like the Armadillo of Thanksgiving Future?" I asked.

Bartleby paused. I bumped into him again.

He said, "Armadillo? What's an armadillo?"

Bartleby was endlessly frustrating.

After a long moment of silence, Bartleby burst out in laughter.

I, on the other hand, did not.

LE CLUB SOUTERRAIN NOCTURNE

It starts at a going-away party.

I hadn't realized how hot and stuffy it was inside Bartleby's tunnel until a lick of cool fresh air washed over my damp face and arms. And when Bartleby stopped crawling forward, and we took in this new sensation, I could also hear the gentle sound of trickling water.

And then there was music. Not the kind of music that came down the well from all the people who'd gathered above me, playing guitars and singing folk songs. This music crackled faintly through a tinny radio speaker that was tuned to a gospel station from Fort Worth.

The song playing was unmistakable—it had been ingrained in my memory since before I could speak. The voice of the singer was my great-grandmother, Lily Abernathy's, and the song playing was "I Will Walk with Him in the Garden of Blood."

Bartleby whispered, "You hear that, Sam?"

I said, "That's my great-grandmother."

"Ha ha! I know that! Isn't it great?" Bartleby asked.

"Um. But why? What's it for?"

Bartleby turned around and grinned, which was the exact same expression an armadillo would have if it weren't grinning. He said, "It's a party. For you! It's your *Going-Away Party*!"

And when Bartleby said "Going-Away Party," his eyes seemed to grow to twice their size and he made jittery jazz hands with his front claws.

I still did not get how Bartleby could be so certain I was going away, not to mention that he seemed to know everything about me and my great-grandmother, but I was kind of touched that he'd arranged to have a party for me.

"Now, this might be a tight squeeze for you, but once you're through we can finally get this party started! We've been waiting for so long," Bartleby said. Then he grunted and pushed himself forward into a narrow slash that cut through a jagged rock wall.

Once Bartleby was inside, the sound of the music and the water became louder, and the cool air increased to a steady breeze on my face, as though Bartleby had been a cork that unstopped whatever was seeping into his tunnel from the other side of the narrow crawl space.

I pushed my head up into the fissure in the rock.

I said, "You're not going to trap me down here, are you?"

"Ha ha!" Bartleby laughed. "You can't trap a trapped rat!"

I shook my head. "I don't know."

Bartleby, at the other end of the doorway (if you could call it that), said, "After all we've been through together, Sam, you still don't trust me? Remember, unicorns never do bad things to little boys. Come on! It's a party—*for you!*"

Well. Everyone likes parties. And I did miss the entire Thanksgiving thing that had supposedly happened at home up above. So I squeezed my shoulders into the opening and belly-crawled, scraping my way in after Bartleby.

The doorway hole was only about as long as I was tall, and once my head and arms had gotten through to the other side, I saw a sparkling cavern that looked like a scene in a fantasy fairy tale come to life before my eyes.

"A cave," I said.

The cavern itself was massive. It was a view I had only seen before in pictures or on television programs about the world's most spectacular caves. Once I'd squeezed through the doorway, the floor dropped down below me and the ceiling vaulted at least twenty feet over my head.

I could stand up again.

All across the ceiling extended thin, fingerlike stalactites that resembled bony icicles, twisting down at me. Some of them had to be nearly ten feet long. And up from the floor rose bulky stalagmites that looked like the rounded bottom teeth of whales or dinosaurs.

"We've been swallowed, Sam! We're inside the mouth of *Planet Earth*! Ha ha! Welcome to Le Club Souterrain Nocturne!" Bartleby cheered.

And when Bartleby said "Le Club Souterrain Nocturne," his eyes (as you have probably come to expect) grew nearly to the size of tangerines, he extended his front claw gracefully like he was some kind of showroom model, and he pointed at a buzzing neon sign that said this:

LE CLUB SOUTERRAIN NOCTURNE

(TRANSLATION FOR OUR NON-FRENCH-SPEAKING

PATRONS: SUBTERRANEAN NOCTURNAL CLUB)

And in the expanse of the cavern ahead of me on the right lay a glimmering pool of perfectly clear water. On the floor of the pool were table-size flat rocks that stairstepped away into a deep-blue, seemingly bottomless lake below. The pool was fed by a waterfall that splashed down from some invisible dark place above us. Along the edge of the small lake, on the left, was a broad, smooth limestone floor.

This was where all the animals were dancing, if you could call it that.

What I mean is this: "I Will Walk with Him in the Garden of Blood" is not the most danceable tune you could ever hear (but it was the only tune that played—over and over and over—from the little red plastic radio sitting on top of one of the nubby stalagmites). The awkwardness of Great-Grandma's song was magnified by the fact that the arms and legs of foxes, prairie dogs, snapping turtles, coyotes, and otters are not very well suited to the articulation of dance movements. But there were all these animals here, dancing and dancing, not one of them seemingly the least bit concerned about their lack of ability, or about a small four-year-old boy who was covered in mud and grime and just standing there in their presence, taking in all the strangeness of the spectacle.

But it was a real party, and for the first time since I'd fallen into the well (and how many days I'd been there I couldn't tell anymore), I felt almost like I wanted to stay here.

And I was suddenly aware of how intensely thirsty I was.

I wanted that water.

I took a few steps toward the edge of the pool and looked down into it. Fish, frogs, and crayfish darted around before me, back and forth like shooting stars from rock to rock, almost as though they were also dancing underwater. I got down onto my knees and dipped my hands into the water.

"Can I drink this?" I asked.

Bartleby hopped from one hind foot to the other. He said, "Ha ha, Sam! There's nothing a subterranean nocturnal animal can't do if he wants to do it! Am I right?"

And then from all above us came a chorus of shrill, squeaky voices: "You're a subterranean nocturnal animal!"

I hadn't even noticed that up among the trunks of the stalactites was a gathering of thousands of bats—all of them, as always, saying exactly the same thing at exactly the same time.

They were also all quivering, dancing to the gospel music, hanging upside down from the ceiling with their tiny feet.

I got down onto my belly at the edge of the water and dipped my face into it. Nothing had ever tasted or felt so good in my short life; it was better than every Thanksgiving pie ever made.

I drank and drank, and all the animals danced and laughed while my great-grandmother sang her morbid song about guilt and horticulture.

When I was full, I sat up and took off my one remaining shoe and sock and I put my feet down into the water. Bartleby came up behind me and started grunting as he pressed his front claws into my shoulder and pushed.

"What are you trying to do?" I said.

"Ugh. Ugh! A joke. It's just a joke. I'm trying to push you into the water, but you're too heavy," Bartleby said. "It's a joke. It's like a tradition at going-away parties. Right? Push the guest of honor into the pool. You don't happen to have a pack of cigarettes or a cell phone in your pocket, do you? Ha ha! Because, you know, water. Ha ha!"

Bartleby kept pushing and grunting.

"Do you throw a lot of going-away parties?" I asked.

"Only this one," Bartleby said. "But it's been going on nonstop since 1888. We originally started the party for Ethan Pixler, the bank robber. Then nobody wanted to go home, so we all just kept it up, *around the clock*!"

And when Bartleby said "around the clock," his eyes got big and his little claws drew circles in the air over my right shoulder.

Bartleby pushed again, harder. He said, "For all the rest of us here know, *you* are Ethan Pixler, and it's about time you showed up! Ha ha!"

"Ethan Pixler! Ethan Pixler!" cried the bats.

Originally, Ethan Pixler never made it to Bartleby's party, due to a scheduling conflict with the State of Texas.

"Ugh!" Bartleby gave another strong push, and then a pair of otters who'd been watching us came over to help him. I didn't mind if it meant I would willingly participate in a traditional going-away party joke; I knew I could use a trip through a washing machine anyway.

The otters spoke Spanish, and very quickly—so fast that I could only make out a few words, which pretty much anyone in Texas can understand. But I could pick out the words for *water* and *push*, as well as a Spanish pronunciation of the name Ethan Pixler.

So I went into the pool with all my clothes on (except for one shoe and one sock that I'd lost, and the other shoe and sock that I'd removed), until the water was over my head, and I swam out into the middle of the glassy lake, which quickly clouded up with mud on account of how filthy I was.

The animals all clapped and laughed.

The bats shrieked, "Ethan Pixler is taking a bath! Ethan Pixler is taking a bath!"

And my great-grandmother sang:

> On my passing I will walk in a garden
> Awash with the blood that grants heaven's pardon.
> A fragrant rose from ev'ry sin I've committed
> Will bloom and sing out, "This sinner's been acquitted."
> Oh, the garden of blood! Oh, the garden of blood!
> I will walk with Him in the garden of blood!

Again, not nearly as fun as "Deep in the Heart of Texas," but I didn't think most of the animals at the party could clap, on account of their front arms being so stubby, and not having shoulders or palms, and so on.

When I climbed out from the pool, I was finally clean, but also completely soaked. And for the first time since I'd fallen into that (excuse me) stupid hole after (excuse me) dumb James Jenkins threw the ball too high when we were playing (excuse me) idiotic Spud, I felt good, and happy, too. But as soon as I realized how nice this all was, I was sad all over again, just thinking about what Mom and Dad were going through in the world up above.

I began to wonder if I'd ever be able to do anything at all in my life and not have my parents suffer because of it. After all, my mother cried for days when I started preschool.

She even cried when Dad took the training wheels off my bike for the first time.

And while everyone else danced and the music continued on an endless loop, Bartleby saw that there was something new that was making me unhappy.

"You should be having a good time, Sam!" Bartleby said. "Why aren't you dancing? Why such a long face? You're not an armadillo! Ha ha! I'm the one with the long face! Ha ha! Get it, Sam? Get it? Long face? Armadillo? Do I need to draw you a picture?"

I sighed. "I'm just— I'm afraid my mom and dad are worried and sad."

Bartleby straightened up. His eyes became serious and narrow slits of black glass.

"Sam," Bartleby scolded, "you are NOT responsible for other people's happiness or sadness. Perhaps you need to spend a few more weeks down here so I can help you straighten out all this growing-up nonsense, because that's what it is. Nonsense. But for now I think you need an *attitude adjustment*!"

And when Bartleby said "attitude adjustment," his voice got dreamy and soft and his eyes opened up again. Then he snapped his front claws like a castanet and called out, "Server! Can this boy get a server, please? Is this a party or a dentist's waiting room? Come on, folks!"

Through the crowded dance floor came a slender golden coyote with long, graceful legs. The coyote seemed to be smiling at me, but coyotes never aren't smiling, I think. And there was some kind of table strapped to the back of the coyote, so when she stopped beside me I could see the table was filled with chocolate cupcakes and glasses of ice-cold milk.

The coyote, grinning because that's what coyotes do, said, "Would you like some refreshments, Mr. Pixler?"

"Oh, thank you. But I'm not Ethan Pixler," I said. "My name's Sam Abernathy."

The coyote hunched down and squinted, her eyes shifting suspiciously from side to side, because that's also what coyotes do. Then she snatched up the shoe I'd taken off and started to slink away with it (because coyotes do stuff like that, too.)

Bartleby snapped, "Hey! Where are you going with that shoe? Put it down!"

The coyote turned into a little wadded-up ball of guilt, her tail curled tightly forward between her legs. She lowered her head almost as though she thought it would make her invisible, but she still kept my shoe in her teeth.

"Audrey," Bartleby warned, "put down the shoe."

Audrey, the coyote, dropped my shoe and raised her head as though she had no idea what had just happened. Her tail stayed put between her legs.

Coyotes, like most dogs, generally feel guilty about something their instincts drive them to do.

I ate two cupcakes and drank three glasses of milk from the serving tray on the back of Audrey, the very friendly and polite but sneaky coyote. When I was finished, I told Audrey thank you very much, and she offered to lick the frosting and milk mustache off my face. I thought that was nice of her, but also a little disgusting, so I told her maybe not this time.

"Okay. Well, back to work for me!" Audrey said.

And when she wandered off through the crowd of dancing animals, I noticed that my shoe was missing, and that Audrey, who was just disappearing behind a circle of dancing jackrabbits, was carrying it off in her teeth.

So much for trusting coyotes, no matter how polite they are!

Tink tink tink!

Tink tink tink!

Everything got quiet. The dancers and music stopped.

Bartleby tapped his claw onto the side of an empty milk glass and cleared his throat.

Tink tink tink!

"Folks! Folks! Our *guest of honor* has finally arrived!"

And when Bartleby said "guest of honor," his eyes grew so large, they nearly swallowed his entire face, and he waved his empty milk glass slowly toward me.

Then he added, "Speech! Speech!"

"Speech! Speech!" squealed the bats on the ceiling.

Nothing is as quiet as the quiet inside an underground cavern when a thousand sets of ears are waiting for you to say something noteworthy.

"Um? Sam?" Bartleby said.

"What am I supposed to do?" I whispered.

"Give your speech," Bartleby whispered back.

"I don't *have* a speech," I argued in a whisper.

"Nobody will notice, as long as you say something *incredibly clever*," Bartleby pointed out.

And when Bartleby said "incredibly clever," well . . . you know the rest.

ROBBING BANKS WITH A FLATBREAD

"I'd like to start by saying that I have never given a speech before.

"Well, not unless you count talking to other four-year-olds at preschool for show-and-tell as giving a speech.

"And I'm afraid I have nothing to show you, and therefore nothing to tell you about—so let me simply say thank you to—"

One of the otters who'd helped Bartleby push me into the water raised his (or her—with otters it's impossible to tell) front paw urgently and said, "Ooh! Ooh!"

"Yes?" I asked.

The otter said this: *"Cuéntanos una historia sobre el robo de un banco!"*

I froze.

I said, "Um."

The otter repeated himself (or herself), slowly, deliberately, like he (or she) was talking to an (excuse me) idiot. *"Cuéntanos una historia sobre el robo de un banco!"*

Audrey, the polite and very sneaky coyote who had small bits of my shoe that she'd chewed to pieces stuck to her snout, said, "He wants you to tell us a story about robbing banks!"

Apparently, Audrey was not just polite and sneaky, she also liked to eat shoes and spoke several languages.

I cleared my throat, buying time to explain myself. After waiting more than a century for my (or whoever's) arrival, the animals here in the underground party had understandably come to expect certain things from their guest of honor, and I was unsure how to proceed, fearful that I would disappoint them.

It was, after all, the first speech I had ever in my life had to give, and I did not want to fall into a hole, so to speak.

"I don't know what to say," I whispered to Bartleby.

Bartleby gave me an armadillo grin, which was not actually a grin so much as it was Bartleby's attempt at ventriloquism. Through his teeth, he whispered, "Just tell them anything at all that you like to do, and then pretend it's the same thing as robbing a bank."

I cleared my throat again.

I began, "Last month, when I visited my aunt and uncle in Plano, they allowed me to make myself an olive and soppressata flatbread for lunch. . . ."

"Which you then used to rob a bank?" Audrey shouted from somewhere in the crowd.

"He robbed a bank with an olive and soppressata flatbread!" shrieked the bats.

"From scratch?" snapped a snapping turtle.

The snapping turtle looked angry, but it could have been mostly my own prejudicial reaction to his appearance. Also, as with otters, I could not tell if the snapping turtle was a boy or a girl, so I'm just going with my instinct and guessing the snapping turtle was a boy turtle.

"Um. Yes, I made it from scratch," I said. "I started off by—"

"Was it gluten-free?" the snapping turtle blurted out. His gums made clicking sounds.

I said, "Huh?"

"Gluten-free!" snapped the snapping turtle, who apparently was not known for lengthier, more descriptive comments.

"Gluten-free!" echoed the bats.

And Audrey, the coyote, said, "*Gluten* is a general name for the proteins found in grass-related grains, such as wheat."

Not only was she polite and sneaky, Audrey also enjoyed eating shoes, was multilingual, and knew a lot of stuff about life.

"You can't rob a bank with a gluten-free soppressata flatbread!" argued an as-yet-unheard-from contentious jackrabbit.

"Ethan Pixler could do it!" shouted a prairie dog with chocolate frosting on his face.

"*Ethan Pixler puede hacerlo!*" agreed the otter.

The bats echoed, "Ethan Pixler!"

It was crazy.

And just as all the animals were building into a frenzy of

excited arguments about gluten and bank robbery, Bartleby raised his armadillo claws and said, "Music! Music! Let's dance!"

The little radio came back on.

My great-grandmother's twangy voice began again.

Then everything shook and rumbled like the world was collapsing in on us.

I had never experienced an earthquake before, but this must be one, I thought. Everything rattled. The walls of the cave moaned deep complaints about the suddenness of change—but that's exactly what you'd expect from rocks.

And Bartleby's eyes narrowed. His shoulders, if he had any, hunched together.

Bartleby said, "They're here for you, Sam! They made it!"

And the bats said, "They made it!"

EIGHTH GRADE

THE HIGHEST AND THE LOWEST POINTS IN BLUE CREEK

Dad didn't start talking to me again for nearly a week following that rainy survival campout.

Unsurprisingly, he caught a terrible cold and was bedridden for the first few days after we got back. But everyone could tell there was something more than a cold that kept Dad from being his usual filler-in of all the blanks.

It was a definite low point for us.

And I felt awful, but there was no going back. Like gravity combined with an unseen hole that gapes open in the path ahead of my footsteps, once I had gone there, all I could do was hope for some kind of soft landing.

It was a lot for Dad to deal with. In fact, the morning after we ate boiled worms in the downpour, one of the first things Dad said to me when we woke up from not actually sleeping was, "You were joking about not wanting to go to MIT, right, Sam?"

But I had to admit the truth and tell him that no, I was not joking—that I really, truly, did not enjoy anything at all that involved math or science, and that I knew what I really wanted to do more than anything else. I told Dad that I wanted to learn the culinary arts. I wanted to be a chef—maybe even a famous one who could be on television, like Resa O'Hare.

And Dad just shook his head. He poked a damp stick into the embers of our fire, trying to prod some energy from it. It was drizzly and gray in the morning, and Dad said, "I don't know what I'm going to do with you, Sam."

If Mom and Dad were a separate country, "I don't know what I'm going to do with you, Sam" would be their official motto. It would be in Latin, in a gold ribbon across the bottom of their flag or something.

Nescio quid facturus sum tecum Sam

"The only future for our world is math and science. It's the only opportunity for success and happiness you'll have, Son."

I didn't tell him that he seemed to be doing just fine, success-wise, despite the fact that he was a kilt-wearing, miniature golf course–owning Texan who neither spliced genes nor calculated near misses with asteroids, and who also ate garbage out of used beer cans.

Then he said, "I guess we should clean up after ourselves and hike out to where Mom said she'd meet up with us."

Those were the last things he said to me that morning. And that was pretty much the last thing he said to me for about five days.

For a while I felt like Dad would never snap out of his moping around. He didn't need to say it outright: I had shattered his dreams, even though they weren't actually his dreams, but were more like a cloud of bad-smelling air that followed us around everywhere, and that he expected me to breathe in and enjoy.

It made me sad to think how all of a sudden, at eleven years old, I had forced my father to confront the reality that I had formed my own ideas about the way things should work out for me, even if I might make mistakes trying.

Blue Creek Days are always held just before Halloween. The date has something to do with the traditional time for planting onion seeds in Texas. Traditionally, onion growing had been a major factor in the settling of Blue Creek, since the area around our town was at one time famous for growing onions, as opposed to being famous for having four-year-old boys who get trapped inside abandoned wells.

With just a little more than a week to go, I took advantage of every opportunity I could to experiment with different interpretations of macaroni and cheese at Karim's house, and tried to avoid my dad as much as possible. Hayley Garcia and the rest of the Science Club kids worked on setting up a display and assembling our experiment for picking up and recording low-frequency rogue radio communications signals, which she had hypothesized were long-running (possibly successful) attempts at interactions with alien cultures.

Karim suggested that we combine the activities. He said there would be no more effective way to invite space aliens to Blue Creek than by offering up some quality macaroni and cheese.

I was nervous about the whole thing. What if I didn't do my best? What if my food ended up being disgusting—and everything I thought I loved doing turned out to be a complete failure?

"This. This is the highest point in Blue Creek," Hayley Garcia said. She placed a computer printout of the town on the table in Mr. Mannweiler's classroom, her fingertip stabbing the precise target for our experiment. "Right here would be the best location for gathering the data for our project."

Michael Dolgoff looked bored. This all happened in our Science Club meeting on Wednesday afternoon. Earlier, Michael Dolgoff had campaigned to reintroduce the bug gladiatorial arena. He told us how he'd recently conducted a cage match between a centipede and a wolf spider. The wolf spider got away in his house, so Michael Dolgoff's mother took away his television, computer, and cell phone.

Karim and Bahar studied the point on Hayley Garcia's map where she'd pinned her index finger. No place in Blue Creek struck any of us as being particularly higher in elevation than anywhere else, but where Hayley was pointing did surprise some of us.

Bahar said, "That's right where Lily Putt's is."

ANDREW SMITH

"Exactly," affirmed Hayley Garcia, who was president, despot, and Minister of the Department of Crackpot Theories for our club. And she added, "To be precise, the highest point in Blue Creek is at the top of the head of the T. rex hazard, which is located at hole thirteen."

It kind of made me feel proud that the highest point in Blue Creek was at the top of our fake dinosaur's head in my family's miniature golf course, and that possible conversations with extraterrestrial civilizations could be taking place inside his hollow fiberglass skull, but I wasn't sure why.

SUNDAY MORNING BISCUITS AND GRAVY

This starts with a computer search and pretending to be someone I am probably not allowed to pretend to be.

I'll be honest: Dad was not the only one who wasn't quite himself the week following our last survival disaster. I was a mess. And it only had a little to do with feeling guilty about telling Dad I was not happy about devoting the rest of my life to physics or whatever subject he thought was going to navigate the ship of my future. I was also very anxious about coming up with a dish that would convincingly win Kenny Jenkins's (excuse me) dumb Blue Creek Days Macaroni and Cheese Cook-Off Challenge.

And on top of everything else, one thing I still couldn't figure out that was bothering me more than anything else for nearly a week now was this: James Jenkins.

My head was filled with questions, and even if the answers seemed sensible to me, they didn't hold up with the James Jenkins myth that everyone in Blue Creek had collectively constructed for the past seven years.

I mean, why was James Jenkins nice to me? Was he really trying to help me when we were stuck in Coach Bovard's torture chamber? Did he actually ask me to come over to his house and hang out with him? Why? Why did he pick *me* to confess to about how much he loved to dance? Why did he show *me* those pictures of himself dancing? What was *I* supposed to do with that information?

I realize you can't ask yourself rhetorical questions, because you're always going to think up instant answers as though you're talking to yourself, which is what I was doing. Because I think I knew the answer to what I was supposed to do with the stuff I'd learned about James Jenkins.

So during the usual time when I'd normally be sneaking in and watching shows about food and cooking on the living room television, I got onto our computer and looked up the dance studio called Acceleration in Austin.

I looked through the school's photo gallery page and found more pictures of James Jenkins there than just the two on the home page. And I also clicked on the link to the "Breaking the Barriers: Austin's Ballet Boy Wonder" newspaper story that appeared in the *Statesman*.

I read the entire feature about James, and once again I was surprised my head did not explode. The reporter who'd written the article obviously spent a lot of time watching James train and talking to him about dance. And if I didn't already know that James Jenkins loved to read and write, some of the things that supposedly came out of his mouth and ended up between quotation marks in the Austin newspaper would have struck me as being complete fiction.

Because in the article, James Jenkins said this: "I think it's time to reexamine the narrative which suggests that dance—ballet in particular—is not a masculine pursuit. The whole idea of discouraging a boy from doing something because fifty or a hundred years ago some uptight white man in America decided it did not fit with the construct of manliness is stupid and offensive."

That was the same James Jenkins who flunked eighth grade, or got *held back*, or whatever else he was told happened to him.

The article made me sad and angry at the same time, and as soon as I finished reading it I made up my mind about what I was going to do.

So I became my father. Well, in name only, because I would never be as into wearing kilts and eating garbage as Dad was. But in that moment, I transformed into Dave Abernathy, the one-time honorary mayor of Blue Creek and owner of Lily Putt's Indoor-Outdoor Miniature Golf Course. Also in that moment, I wished I were better with words, like James Jenkins was, because where did he come up with saying things like "narrative" and "construct" without borrowing a thesaurus from (excuse me) dumb Mr. Mannweiler, who encouraged me to only use "easy" words?

And it took me nearly an hour just to write a one-paragraph e-mail to Acceleration Dance Studio that sounded grown-up enough to have come from a small-business owner named Dave Abernathy, who was inviting the studio to come to Blue Creek Days, and asking specifically, maybe you could have that James Jenkins kid in the newspaper article, you know, the ballet boy wonder (since he comes from Blue Creek and all), and some of his dance partners put on a little demonstration for the people of our little town.

In my (Dad's) e-mail, I even included the following spectacular closing:

> The people of Blue Creek Town love ballet even more
> than we love biscuits and gravy!
> Sincerely,
> Dave Abernathy
> Owner, Lily Putt's Indoor-Outdoor Miniature Golf Course
> Honorary Mayor of Blue Creek, 2015–2016

I realize it was laying things on a bit thick, because getting between a Blue Creeker and his Sunday morning biscuits and gravy was like trying to get between a pair of cubs and their grizzly-bear mom: You were bound to end up with tooth marks. But I was hoping for my (Dad's) enthusiasm to convince Acceleration Dance Studio to surprise us all with something nobody in our town would ever have expected.

I for one never expected what ended up happening as a result of what I did.

THE MUSTANG MILE

"Are you trying to start something?" James Jenkins asked.

Let me explain.

First off, it was difficult for me to answer him because I was afraid that I was about to be murdered. And again I found myself in the precarious position of potentially being murdered no matter how I answered James's question. Thirdly, it was hard to say anything on account of the fact that James Jenkins had my back pinned beside the doorway of the (excuse me) stupid boys' locker room, and I was pretty sure he was about to punch me, and I have never been punched by anyone in my life.

Also, I was worried because we only had three minutes to change into our PE clothes, James Jenkins was using up precious non-talking and non-gum-chewing getting-dressed time, and trouble just seemed to always find me and James Jenkins when it came to the locker room, PE class, and Coach Bovard.

I had grossly miscalculated James Jenkins's reaction to my e-mail invitation for his dance school to come out to Blue Creek and have James give the town a show. And I could see by

James's expression that he was afraid. It also looked like he was on the verge of crying, and one thing you never want to do to a murderer is make him cry in front of you, because a crying murderer is probably the most scary kind of murderer that ever existed.

"I . . . I'm sorry . . . Um. James. I thought it was something you wanted to do," I said. My words didn't even sound convincing to me, though.

James Jenkins didn't say anything. He just inhaled—deeply and very slowly—through his nose, like a sad murderer would do. His face was red and his eyes were wet.

So, taking advantage of the delay in my being murdered, I continued, "Really, James. When I saw those pictures, and you told me how much you love to do ballet, and then I even read that article about you in the *Statesman*, I thought it would be cool if you could show us all what you do. I thought you'd be happy. I'm really sorry."

"I almost believed you were starting to be nice to me after all this time. I thought we were friends or something," James Jenkins said.

I felt sick in my stomach when I saw a tear squeeze out from the corner of James Jenkins's unmoving right eye. I looked down so I wouldn't have to see him.

Why was James Jenkins apparently needing me to be nice to him? There was something—and it must have been pretty big—that I was missing.

I felt terrible.

I never intended to do something *bad* to James Jenkins, but I guess it happened.

James softened and I looked at him. It almost felt like he'd given up or something. He took his hands away from my shoulders, even though I fully expected (and believed I deserved) to be punched by James Jenkins.

Guys began coming out from the locker room, dressed for PE.

The bug kid—Michael Dolgoff—stopped, looked at us, and shook his head.

(Excuse me.) "You guys are so freakin' stupid," Michael Dolgoff said.

Another boy, named Brody Bjork, said (excuse me), "If Blovard makes us run, I'm kicking your ass, Abernathy."

Brody Bjork was a *Mathlete*, so I didn't take his threat too seriously, which was probably one of many mistakes I'd made since coming back from my rain-soaked worm-eating vacation with Dad.

Talk about putting on a show for Blue Creek!

A third kid, named Malaki Jackson, who had a very high-pitched, piercing voice, said (excuse me), "Holy jeez! Abernathy made JJ cry!"

And that was it. I deserved to be murdered. Worse than murdered, if there was such a thing.

James (JJ, as Malaki and some of the other boys at Dick

Dowling Middle School called him) swiped a palm across his face and without saying anything else ducked (very slowly) into the locker room, leaving me standing there alone in front of an audience of the entire eighth-grade boys' PE class. I calculated (and not being a *Mathlete* like Brody Bjork, I was probably wrong) that I had less than a minute to change into my (excuse me) idiotic PE uniform, so I dashed through the doorway after James Jenkins.

I was already half undressed by the time I made it to my locker. But James Jenkins had not finished dressing, and although it was certain that we were not about to say anything to each other, the bell rang for us to be in our numbered spots for Coach Bovard to do his head count.

James Jenkins and I were late to class, and Coach Bovard was standing at the end of our bench, his arms folded across his chest, just watching us. Or, at least, it *looked* like he was watching us. It was hard to tell.

Coach Bovard had a clipboard tucked under one arm and was wearing sunglasses that were so dark, you couldn't tell what he was looking at or if his eyes were even open. "I don't know what it is with you two," he said, shaking his head. Then Coach Bovard added, "I think the whole class is going to be so happy to run the Mustang Mile today."

My heart sank to my belly button.

Nobody was ever happy about doing the Mustang Mile, which was actually much longer (and more difficult) than a regular mile.

The Mustang Mile was four laps on the track, like a regular mile, but at each of the long straightaways we had to go up and down every stairway on both the home-side and visitor-side bleachers—all the way to the top and then back down to the bottom. There were eight staircases on the home side and six on the other, plus a mile on the track, on top of everything.

And of all the boys in our class, not one of them seemed to connect our punishment with anything James Jenkins did—it was all on me. They all wanted to kill me, but I probably deserved it, anyway.

As was the usual case on our class runs, I was next to last, and James Jenkins was just a few steps behind me. It was especially frightening because of the noise of all those feet thundering up and down the aluminum bleachers in front of me, and then the pursuing *clank! clank! clank!* of James Jenkins's size twelves slowly and steadily trailing along just behind me, that sounded like some kind of tireless, mechanized metallic murderer.

On the fifth staircase up the home side on our final lap, James Jenkins got closer. And then closer.

My legs were burning. I was too little to take such big steps, and as much as I desperately did not want James Jenkins to catch up to me, I couldn't speed up to get away from him.

I started humming "I Will Walk with Him in the Garden of Blood."

Pretty soon, James Jenkins was right beside me, matching

my stride, step for step. He kept his chin and eyes forward.

James Jenkins said, "My instructor at Acceleration called me before lunch today and asked me if I'd dance for her. That's how I knew it had to be you. I can't say no to my instructor."

There was nothing I could say to him. I kept my eyes down so I wouldn't see how many steps were still ahead of me.

Clank! Clank! Clank! Clank!

James Jenkins kept his eyes forward. But that was just because he's James Jenkins. He said, "Why did you do that? My dad's never going to let me go back to my mom's place now."

Clank! Clank! Clank! Clank!

My eyes stung from sweat, and my lungs strained for oxygen, but I managed to choke out, "Are you going to kill me, James?"

James Jenkins didn't answer for a really long time, which is totally something a murderer who was running the Mustang Mile and who also didn't really want his dad to see him dance would do in response to a question like that. We had gotten to the top, then turned and headed back down the opposite side of the stairs. Only three more staircases to go—and then we'd have to do the visitors' side.

(Excuse me.)

And James Jenkins said, "I'm not going to kill you, Sam. But maybe Brody Bjork or Malaki Jackson will."

I looked across to the opposite bleachers. Brody Bjork and Malaki Jackson were already at the bottom of the last staircase on the visitors' side—the finish line for Coach Bovard's (excuse me) Moronic Mustang Mile. They had their shirts off and were doubled over, their hands on their knees, breathing hard, sweating, exhausted.

They'd certainly be rested and fresh, and ready to kill me, by the time I got to the bottom of that final staircase.

James and I finished the home-side bleachers and went back out onto the track to round the bend to the visitors' side. There were only a few guys still running ahead of us, and James was right beside me, so close I could feel the heat radiating from his body like a cloud of volcanic vapors. He continued to match my pace without saying another word.

We got to the top of the first staircase on the last set of bleachers, and as we turned to head back down I said, "Do you want me to tell them to cancel it? My dad, I mean. I mean pretend to be my dad and then tell them not to come? And to not make you do ballet? At Blue Creek Days? So you don't have to do it? Because I will, if you want. Do you want me to do that? Tell them no?"

I knew what I said made absolutely no sense, but I hoped James understood what I was offering to do.

I counted the clangs of our footsteps while James Jenkins was not answering me. On the way up the second set, James finally said, "No."

I was so happy James Jenkins answered me, and that I was still alive—at least until I got in with the rest of the boys.

"Do you mean tell them no? Or you don't want me to tell them no?" I asked.

"Will you just shut up?" James Jenkins said.

Now I was confused, but I was also too scared of James Jenkins to say anything else.

At the bottom again, James finally cleared things up. He said, "I want to do it, but just shut up."

I took a deep breath. "Okay," I said. "I'm shutting up."

James did not move his head. He never did. He just kept his focus forward as though he were intensely concentrating on the finest details of every single one of those (excuse me) stupid aluminum stairs.

And as we turned to climb up the last set, and every sweaty, angry, out-of-breath boy in our class was at the bottom, waiting, watching us, James Jenkins said, "Just stay by me so those guys don't start messing with you."

So I said, "I think it's time to reexamine the narrative which suggests that the construct of manliness encourages boys to punch other boys they get mad at for making them run Mustang Miles."

And James Jenkins, without moving his eyes or his chin, said, "Shut up, Sam."

A DAY FOR GROSS MISCALCULATIONS

The worst things start with the end-of-the-school-day bell.

I realized that I came very near to ruining James Jenkins's life, and it was all because I had assumed I was so smart about things that I could easily solve all his problems. But that was incredibly (excuse me) stupid of me, and it made me feel awful.

So I did what James Jenkins suggested, and I just shut up for the rest of the day.

I also stayed on an imaginary James Jenkins leash that was about eighteen inches long when we all went back into the locker room and the extremely (excuse me) disgusting showers. Nobody would get near me as long as I hung around James Jenkins, and that only worsened my feelings of guilt, on account of the fact that I was taking advantage of James being so frightening to the other boys (and to me).

But if anyone had the right to be mad enough to punch me in the face, it was James Jenkins who should be in the front of that line.

Still, as creepy as it was, it seemed like all the guys in our

PE class, including Brody Bjork, Malaki Jackson, and (excuse me) dumb Michael Dolgoff, just stared at me the whole time I was in the shower, like a pack of murderers would do, or like hungry lions who were just waiting for the extremely adorable and tiny baby antelope to lag behind the protection of the herd, which in this case consisted of an intimidating fourteen-year-old ballet boy wonder named James Jenkins.

I really did break the universe.

And once Coach Bovard released us boys from class and we all scattered, limping and sore from our Mustang Mile, in different Dick Dowling directions for the last classes of the day, I assumed that, like most grievances in middle school, everything about what I'd done to get the class punished had been forgotten.

Unfortunately, I was completely wrong about this.

It was a day for gross miscalculations on my part.

Blue Creek Days were nearly upon us, but I hadn't yet decided on a recipe for my entry. Every day after school, I'd been experimenting at Karim's house, and he and Bahar both loyally swore to me that they were *not* getting tired of daily variations of macaroni and cheese. But that's what friends do, I suppose, as opposed to tricking you into performing ballet in front of a bunch of red-meat-craving Texas football fans, or throwing a ball in such a way that it causes you to wind up trapped for three days in an abandoned well.

Hayley Garcia and the rest of the Science Club were nearly

finished assembling our rogue-radio-station alien-monitoring device, and they were counting on me to climb up the fiberglass T. rex at Lily Putt's Indoor-Outdoor Miniature Golf Course (the highest point in Blue Creek) that weekend to perform the installation. I just hoped Dad wasn't planning on proclaiming "kilt day" at the golf course. But I wouldn't know anyway, because Dad wasn't saying much to me these days.

The final bell of the day rang and the main hallway of Dick Dowling Middle School transformed into a swirling sea of bodies, all unaware of the individual missions each of us was on—to get outside the building and breathe freedom once again. It was the way things always went: Nobody paid attention to anyone, because we were all so focused on making the most economical departure possible.

That's the best way I can explain why I did not notice Malaki Jackson, Brody Bjork, and Michael Dolgoff the bug warrior waiting for me in the hall as I went to dump my books into my locker. And while I was caught up in the moment of not paying attention to the epicenter of activity in the hallway, the boys came up from behind me as I had my face pointed into my locker.

I felt just a momentary sensation of fingers gripping my shoulders, then a solid shove from behind, and in less than one second the worst imaginable thing that I could ever think of happened: the boys pushed me inside my locker and slammed the metal door completely shut, trapping me inside.

ANDREW SMITH

I was dimly aware of Malaki Jackson (because he had that high-pitched voice) laughing and saying, "See you in a Mustang Mile or two, Abernathy!"

Then everything went completely black.

HEART-SHAPED CONFIDENCE

This all starts with a memory.

Ever since that Thanksgiving Day when I was four years old, there had been a giant blank spot in the stories my memory constructed about the Little Boy in the Well.

I mean, I had heard so much about those three days and their aftermath that the stories people *told* me painted their own pictures—filled in the blanks—as though they were really what I experienced.

I could not tell the difference.

Even so, I could never recall what even *one second* of being trapped at the bottom of that well actually felt like. I couldn't remember the first thing about my days in the well, or much at all about the year or so after when I simply stopped talking.

I could not bring back any of it, not until the moment those three boys slammed my locker door shut and trapped me inside that small, lightless space. Then it was almost like a movie began playing on the screen of my memory, filling my head with all those sounds, smells, and stories about how it felt being so hopelessly lost when I was such a small kid.

And there was something else, too—something that started with a tap on my hand and a very familiar voice I had neither heard nor thought about for seven years.

"Seems like we only ever meet during unicorn molting season. You know, when my horn falls off."

Then a name popped into my head—one that I hadn't thought of at all since I'd come out of the well.

"Bartleby?" I said.

All these images and feelings came rushing back to me—the memories of being trapped in the well flooded my head. It was like filling a teacup with a firehose: the dirty trick Bartleby played on me when he (excuse me) pooped on my foot, Ethan Pixler's coffin and secret hideout, the wild going-away party in the cave with all the animals.

"It really is me! Really, really, really!" Bartleby said, hopping from one hind foot to the other. "Ha ha, Sam! Look how much you've grown! High-four! Or high-nine! Or whatever! Ha ha!"

Armadillos only have four fingers on their front feet. Or hands. Or whatever they use to high-four with.

And then Bartleby, naturally, went on. "Oh, forget all this math! Just hug me, Sam! It's been a long time!"

Bartleby, I noticed while we were hugging, smelled like rotten garbage.

But he said, "You smell really good, Sam. Like vanilla and spice and bug repellent!"

"It's my—excuse me—stupid solid deodorant, which I had to put on after we did the Mustang Mile and had to take—excuse me—dumb showers," I said.

"Ha ha! Who would ever want to be a human?" Bartleby asked. "Remember how muddy we got when we spent all that time together in the well? Those were good days, Sam. Good days!"

"I didn't remember anything for a long time. I'm just starting to remember it. Just now," I said.

"Well? Remember how I told you if you ever needed me again that I'd be back?" Bartleby said. "Because that's what subterranean nocturnal friends do for each other."

I honestly could not remember Bartleby telling me that. And what I did remember seemed so scrambled, like a movie cut up into segments and rearranged into some incomprehensible disorder.

Bartleby's curly whiskers tickled my face.

He let go of me and stood back at arm's length. Somehow the inside of my locker had transformed into something as big as a bus station waiting room.

Bartleby scratched his chin and said, "Well, guess what, Sam. You might *think* you need me now, but you really don't."

I bit the inside of my lip. "How am I supposed to get out of here?"

"I'll dig us a tunnel!" Bartleby said.

I did not think an armadillo could burrow through steel, but Bartleby was Bartleby, after all. "You will?" I asked.

ANDREW SMITH

"Ha ha! No! Of course not. We are encased in *solid steel*!"

Bartleby's eyes gleamed. He said, "You're never *not* going to be the Little Boy in the Well."

"I figured as much," I admitted.

"Yeah? Well, guess what, Sam. You're also never going to be without people who care about you too. People who *love you*."

Bartleby made a heart shape between his front claws, which were really quite ugly to look at.

But I didn't exactly feel Bartleby's heart-shaped confidence.

And Bartleby said, "How's the macaroni and cheese coming along? Are you going to win?"

I shook my head. Bartleby knew everything about me. He always did.

"I don't know," I said.

"Just remember to use the *secret ingredient*," Bartleby said.

And when Bartleby said "secret ingredient," his eyes flared open like magnolia blossoms in late spring and he hooked his front claws into air quotes. It was something I could not remember, but had also never forgotten, after all those years.

I asked, "What's the *secret ingredient*?"

I made air quotes too.

And Bartleby, being Bartleby, said, "You never told me! You're keeping it secret! Remember, Sam? Ha ha ha!"

Bartleby was so annoying. *That* I could remember.

Then came a rattling sound, and Bartleby said, "Well, I'll be seeing you, Sam. Don't forget what I said!"

"Forget *what*?" I asked.

But it was too late. Before the words even came out of my mouth, Bartleby vanished into the darkness.

Blinding light flooded into the small space of my locker, and then there were hands again, grabbing at me.

Somebody pulled me out of the dark and into the fluorescent light and linoleum of the main hallway at Dick Dowling Middle School. I nearly tripped over my feet and had to brace myself against the wall of lockers to keep from falling down. I was dizzy, gasping for air, and blinded as though I may have been trapped inside the locker for days. I had no idea how long it had been since those boys had slammed me in there.

Maybe it was three days.

"I told you to watch out for those guys. Are you okay?"

It was James Jenkins who opened my locker and pulled me out. He had his hand on my shoulder and was staring into my blank and unfocused eyes. I didn't answer him. I just stood there, looking around the hallway, which was already completely empty of kids.

James repeated himself. "Sam, are you okay? Can you even hear me?"

"How long was I in there?" I asked.

"About three seconds. That's it. Those guys took off when they saw me coming. Do you need to go to the nurse or anything? You look like you're sick or something."

And that's when I (excuse me) threw up all over our shiny

and clean Dick Dowling Mustangs linoleum hallway. It was also when I witnessed James Jenkins moving faster than I'd ever seen him move in his life as he leapt backward to avoid the splattering torrent of my (excuse me) barf.

Being (excuse me) barfed on by someone else has to be just about as bad as getting trapped in an abandoned well for three days.

THE
LAST
DAY
IN
THE
HOLE

BARTLEBY MAKES A LIST

Everything always starts at the end of a party, or at the bottom of a well, I guess.

The growling roar of the digging machine got louder and louder as Bartleby led me back to my place in the well. It sounded like the entire planet was straining to chew me up and swallow me once and for all. I felt the vibrations coming from the metal teeth of the digger as they tore through the dirt and rock.

It was terrifying, and so loud that Bartleby and I had to scream over the noise just to hear each other. Up above, people were singing and shouting. In all the clamor, I couldn't make out anything specific in their songs and words, but it was the sound of victory. It sounded like a party.

And the little blob of sky looked like polished turquoise.

Bartleby placed a hand on the rock wall beside my shoulder. He said, "Oh my! They're just inches away, Sam. You're going to get out. Happy day! Happy day!"

I watched Bartleby's jittering hand as he pressed it to the wall.

Something very strange was going on inside me: I was not sure that I wanted to leave. In many ways I had become used to being in the well. I even kind of liked it. And I had gotten used to Bartleby and his annoying personality. And I liked the chorus of bats, Ethan Pixler's secret hideout, and especially Audrey, the intelligent and polite coyote.

Bartleby must have noticed the confusion in my eyes.

He said, "What's wrong, Sam?"

"I'm going to leave," I said.

Bartleby's face got as serious as an armadillo's face could get. He said, "Well? You've been wanting to leave since you got here! Don't tell me you'd rather stay down here! I'll never understand you people."

"But what's going to happen to you?"

Bartleby pressed his very thin lips together and shook his head. "To me? To *me?* Just think about what's going to happen to you! You're going to start school next year. One day, you're going to fly in an airplane for the first time. You're going to learn how to tie a necktie and to be someone's *big brother*."

And when Bartleby said "big brother," his eyes got big and wet and he raised his hands over his head like he was showing an invisible Sam Abernathy how to grow up.

Bartleby kept making his list: "You're going to step your bare feet into the ocean one day. You're going to learn how to cook human food, and people are going to love it. People are going to love you, too, Sam—and one day you're even going to fall in love with someone very special. And a long time from now, you're going to be an old man—as old as Ethan Pixler, except with a pulse! Ha ha! You're going to play tricks, and have tricks played right back at you, change a flat tire, get bad haircuts, see scary movies with your friends, make your mom cry on Mother's Day, get in trouble for things you didn't do, and not get caught for things you really did."

Bartleby took a deep breath and wiped his eyes. He was crying. He said, "Do you want to know what else you'll do? You are going to change someone's life, and you will *change the world*, Sam Abernathy!"

I shook my head. I said, "But what about you?"

"What do you mean, what about me?" Bartleby asked.

"Are you just going to go away?"

"Of course not! Ha ha! I'm going to stay down here, living the unicorn life in my subterranean palace, with *all this luxury*, and all my subterranean friends."

And when Bartleby said "all this luxury," he arched his nearly bald eyebrows and fanned his arms out as though he were showing me a beautiful room and a surrounding mass of other subterranean nocturnal animals. Then he turned his pointy armadillo snout toward the tunnel he'd dug near my feet.

The roar of the digging machine was so loud, it hurt my head.

"Wait," I said. "Don't go."

Bartleby stopped, then turned around. He put his little

hands on my face and wiped the mud away from my cheeks. He said, "Aww . . . Don't cry, Sam. I'll always be here for you if you ever need me. Ethan Pixler will too! Ha ha!"

Then Bartleby hugged me and pressed his snout up to my ear and said, "I love you, buddy. Be kind up there, okay? People need kindness as much as they need food to eat. Maybe more."

Bartleby turned around and ducked into his tunnel.

The noise of the digging stopped.

Bartleby's tunnel closed up behind him, like it was never there at all.

A little bit of dirt spilled into the well beside my shoulder.

They had gotten through.

A GREAT LEAP FORWARD

This starts with something I don't think I would have ever realized if it hadn't been for James Jenkins pulling me out of my locker.

It wasn't my fault, and it wasn't James Jenkins's fault either. Because sometimes things just happen, and like Bartleby told me, you can't just live your life with the singular mission of trying to never fall into a hole.

"Sam? Can you hear me? We're there, Son." My dad's voice crackled through the cable. "They're going to see if they can get a man down to you. You're coming home, Son."

I didn't know what I was supposed to do. I was so tired, and I didn't say anything to him. I shut my eyes and started to fall asleep again.

"Sam? Sam? Can you say something, sweetie?" Dad said.

I said, "Okay."

Up above, there was cheering at the sound of my voice coming through the loudspeakers. People were actually thrilled, and all I did was say *okay*.

And I never remembered any of this until that October afternoon seven years later, when I was eleven years old and James Jenkins told me he would walk home with me to make sure I was all right after I'd been slammed inside my locker at Dick Dowling Middle School.

He'd said, "We should get those guys in trouble for what they did to you."

We'd been walking along Pike Street, which was a block north of the school. Behind us, the two-lane strip of cracked asphalt led to Lily Putt's, Colonel Jenkins's Diner, and the center of Blue Creek. Ahead were the open fields and woods and the old spread-out homes that used to be farms where we'd grown up. My nose was a little runny. I kept my chin down and watched the red dirt and gravel that was so familiar as it passed beneath my feet, and all the way I was thinking about those days I'd spent in the well, finally remembering an armadillo who pretended to be a unicorn, a bank robber's coffin, and the strange blindness that overcame me when I was pulled out from the narrow rescue shaft that had been dug for me, *on an angle*, as Bartleby had liked to say.

James Jenkins said, "What's wrong? You're not saying anything."

I didn't look at him.

I said, "I'm sorry if I—excuse me—barfed on your shoes."

James Jenkins never laughed. Why would anyone expect him to? But I knew that if James Jenkins never laughed, it was *not* because he was a murderer. He made a kind of breathy "huh" sound, which was a great leap forward in the evolution of laughter for James Jenkins.

He said, "I got out of the way in time."

"I never saw you move that fast in my life," I said.

James Jenkins made that "huh" sound again.

It was a good sign that maybe James Jenkins would learn how to laugh.

"It's all the ballet," he said.

"You jump good."

"Yeah," James Jenkins said.

The thing is, when they had dug that rescue shaft—*on an angle*—to get me out of the well, they did not take into consideration the size of the firefighter who was supposed to crawl through it in order to reach me. It couldn't be done. The tunnel was too small.

An ominous quiet had fallen over the crowds around the well as it began to sink in that maybe the Little Boy in the Well would not be saved that day. Maybe he would never be saved.

They tried to lower a harness on a cable down for me. I could touch it, and doing that made me feel somehow half-connected to the world above me, but the way I had fallen put me in a position where I could not move my arms enough to pull the harness over me. I tried for an hour before I gave up.

It felt like torture.

For the third day in a row I heard Mom crying through the little speaker.

And Dad kept telling me not to give up, but I knew he was saying it more to all those people up above than he was to me.

The engineers and rescue crews had to regroup and come up with another strategy to save the Little Boy in the Well. Nobody had to tell me, it was obvious from the weight of silence above me, that many of them were beginning to doubt anything would ever work out. They considered making a call out to emergency crews to find the smallest firefighter in Texas, if there was such a thing. Someone suggested contacting a circus contortionist who might be able to dislocate her shoulders in order to squeeze into the rescue shaft.

It was frustratingly ridiculous at that point. I wished Bartleby would come back.

I tried to go to sleep.

And it was during the stall of quiet frustration that a seven-year-old boy named James Jenkins—most people called him Jimmy then—who had been at the top of the well, waiting for three days with his mother and father because he felt so terrible about causing me to fall down that uncovered hole, slipped that yellow nylon harness around his chest and crawled headfirst down the narrow rescue shaft while people shouted for him to stop, and what was he doing, and was he out of his mind, and so on.

I remembered.

When he walked home with me that day in eighth grade, I remembered—I could almost feel exactly what it had felt like when James Jenkins's hand slipped into my little space at the bottom of that well and grabbed on to mine.

I remembered.

BLUE
CREEK
DAYS

THE SIZE OF THE TRUTH

My life starts on Pike Street, walking home with James Jenkins almost exactly seven years after I fell into a hole.

I felt awful about what I had done to James Jenkins.

For seven years I had tried to stay out of holes, and for seven years I had believed things about James Jenkins that were not true.

The time had come for me to reexamine the narrative which suggested that James Jenkins was a murderous, football-playing brute who was entirely to blame for those three days I'd spent at the bottom of an empty well.

That was *not* James Jenkins.

The truth was so much bigger than I had ever estimated it to be.

Blue Creek Days had come. It was a perfect autumn Saturday, a relieving non-camping weekend when maybe fifty years ago all the people around these parts would have been planting onion seeds. And now it seemed they were all filling in blanks, charting out life courses for future football players and computer programmers, and commuting thirty miles in each direction to work inside boxy industrial buildings that seemed to change name and ownership every time the stock market hiccupped.

I got out of bed early so I could prep the macaroni and cheese dish I'd come up with. It was a risk for Blue Creek. Well, it would have been more of a risk for onion-planting Blue Creek than tech-sector Blue Creek. I'd settled on a baked orecchiette in a sauce of Gorgonzola with prosciutto and small bits of caramelized autumn pears. The trick was to get the dish in the oven just late enough in the morning so it would be perfectly done when the judging began at noon.

In the meantime, there was all the last-minute setup for the Science Club. Hayley Garcia and the rest of the kids had mostly come to the conclusion that I was dead weight for not helping out with our project as much as I should have. She theorized that I was only using the prestige of the Science Club to pad my transcript for getting into Blue Creek Magnet School.

Hayley Garcia had no idea how much I did not care about Science Club or Blue Creek Magnet.

Still, they were counting on me to be the one to climb up the T. rex at Lily Putt's Indoor-Outdoor Miniature Golf Course and install the club's receiving unit, which looked like a big tinfoil birthday hat.

And it was always the busiest day of the year at Lily Putt's, which was right across from the main site of Blue Creek Days—

the town's community center. Dad was kilted up and already gone by the time I got out into the kitchen, which was a good thing, because he still wasn't really talking to me for the whole ruining-his-dreams thing about my not wanting to go to MIT.

Then there was the James Jenkins problem. I could tell he'd been very nervous about the dance demonstration, even given that James Jenkins was the kind of kid who just didn't ever show emotions very obviously (and it was NOT because he was a murderer; it was because of so many other things going on in that kid's head, a lot of which I felt responsible for).

I may have been more nervous for James Jenkins than he was for himself. After all, it was my fault that he found himself cornered into performing—even if he ended up telling me he really *wanted* to do it.

And I didn't know if he actually *did* want to do it.

I think James Jenkins was just the kind of kid who didn't say no to people, a kid who never let other people feel let down, even if it meant potentially embarrassing himself—like by performing ballet in front of the formerly onion-planting townsfolk of Blue Creek, and especially in front of his chicken-fried-steak-on-a-stick dad.

At all costs, after what I'd done to him, and after what I finally had remembered James Jenkins had done for me, I'd have to be there for James today—no matter what. I imagined myself transforming into some kind of warrior superhero and running through the crowd, punching people right in the nose for making fun of him, except I don't think I could ever punch anyone in my life.

It all made me extremely anxious, so much that my hands shook as I stirred the cream and gorgonzola into the roux to create the base of my sauce.

"Sam, why are you in the kitchen, cooking in your underwear?" My little sister, Evie, startled me with a surprise entry into my prep.

There were too many subterranean nocturnal animals running around in my brain that morning. I hadn't even bothered to finish getting dressed, I was so flustered. I had intended to put on my official Clan Abernathy kilt that day. As much as I didn't like wearing it in front of people, I hoped it would make Dad happy again. And maybe James Jenkins wouldn't feel entirely alone in the Blue Creek Days Embarrassment Club.

I looked down at my bare legs.

My kilt was still balled up on the floor of my closet.

(Excuse me.)

"Oh my gosh," I said, and ran back to my room.

I was a mess.

THE T. REX WITH THE TINFOIL HAT

This starts at the top of a giant fiberglass T. rex's head.

I was good at climbing the T. rex, and Rigo, who was the only other worker at Lily Putt's who was forced to do it, preferred not to. Hole thirteen, where the giant orange T. rex guarded the carpeted fairway, required golfers to putt their ball into a tunnel between the dinosaur's legs. There were some mechanized feeder tracks inside the thing that would then cause the ball to come spitting out the dinosaur's toothy mouth and drop in the direction of the hole. Sometimes the mechanism would get jammed, and either Rigo or I would have to climb up and reach our arms into the T. rex's throat in order to dislodge the trapped ball.

This time there was no jam. I was climbing the dinosaur to install our receiver unit, a big shiny tin cone connected to a relay that would send whatever we received from outer space, or wherever, over to our club's presentation booth at the fair.

"Holy cow, Sam!" Karim, who was standing beside the T. rex's back foot, said. "Hayley, Bahar, don't look! Turn around!" Then he said (excuse me), "Sam, what the heck are you thinking?"

I was just raising my left foot to step up onto the dinosaur's tiny little arm.

Karim was six feet below, looking at me.

Like I said, it is never really a good idea to climb a T. rex in your kilt, especially if there is an audience of middle schoolers standing beneath you.

(Excuse me.)

"Well, what do you expect? I'm just trying to do my part for our—excuse me—dumb project. And it isn't polite to look up a guy's kilt, in case you didn't know," I said.

I was so flustered; there were a million things firing through my head, and I was completely unconcerned about such things as kilts and spectators, or the highest point in Blue Creek. I positioned the big cone hat on top of the T. rex and flipped the switch for the transmitter. It was all set.

I slid down the spine of the fiberglass dinosaur (which was also not such a good idea in a kilt).

"It looks good," Bahar said.

Karim coughed.

"I mean the receiver-transmitter unit," Bahar clarified. She turned deep red.

"He looks like he's going to a party," I said.

And Hayley Garcia, always organized and executive, said, "And, speaking of which, we should get over to the fair and see how the signal is coming in."

But there were still a few things I had to do, and time was running out. Not bending, not slowing down; it was just running out.

I said, "I'll meet you guys over there. I need to go to the—excuse me—bathroom. See you in a few minutes."

PAS DE DEUX

This starts with a conspiracy of time.

Something was going to be lost.

REALIZATION NUMBER 1: You can't be in two places at the same time.

By the time we (I) had finished with the installation of the giant metal birthday hat on the T. rex, it was already nearly eleven o'clock, and the demonstration from Acceleration and James Jenkins was supposed to begin at eleven.

I was stuck.

If I ran home, I would have enough time to get my macaroni and cheese into the oven and cooked, and then make it back for the judging at noon, but I would have to miss James's dance demonstration. And I couldn't do that to James after what I'd done to make the whole thing happen in the first place.

I had to do the right thing.

There would be other Blue Creek Days. There would be more cooking competitions in the future, maybe even some where I'd have a chance of beating James's nasty and untalented father, Kenny Jenkins. But still, when I came out of the bathroom after getting myself ready to go across to the fair, I was so disappointed with myself, I nearly felt like crying.

"I see you got your club's gadget up on Rusty." My dad caught me just as I was about to leave Lily Putt's. He named our T. rex Rusty, on account of the orange paint on his (or her) bumpy skin. And Dad said, "It's nice to see you in our Clan Abernathy kilt for Blue Creek Days."

He still did not have the usual enthusiasm in his voice.

I nodded, and looked down and said, "Yeah."

"Is there something wrong, Sam?" Dad asked.

"No."

"Did you do your cooking thing?"

And when Dad said "cooking thing," his eyes got smaller and darker, like he was talking about a car accident, or a visit to the doctor.

I felt like a flattened balloon.

I said, "I decided not to do it."

Dad's eyebrows migrated closer together, kind of the way they did when he was looking really hard in bushes for trash we could cook with or eat, but not finding anything there.

There was nothing to find, I thought.

I said, "Um. I really have to go, Dad. I'm supposed to be at *a thing* over there at eleven."

Dad frowned a little, obviously not finding what he was looking for. He said, "Okay," and I dashed across the street to the fair.

I hadn't been to Blue Creek Days in years. I did not like Blue Creek Days for some obvious reasons. First, Blue Creek Days was pretty much a showcase for Kenny Jenkins and Colonel Jenkins's Diner, neither of which I particularly cared for. Worse was the fact that there were still plenty of Blue Creekers—and I saw this virtually every day—who still wore their old PRAY FOR SAM T-shirts.

I hated that.

And as I ran through the people crowding the midway, just as I passed the Science Club booth, where Hayley Garcia was tuning in whatever was out there, I heard someone say, "It's the Little Boy in the Well!" Another person said, "Hey! It's Pray for Sam! Look how small he still is!" And the inevitable "That boy's wearing a dress!"

(Excuse me.)

I didn't care. It was eleven, and I could hear someone testing the microphone at the main stage, talking about the dance school that'd come out to Blue Creek Days, all the way from Austin.

So much for macaroni and cheese.

By the time I worked my way to the front of the stage, there was a young woman at the microphone who introduced herself as Miss Olga. She had a thick accent that made her sound like a spy, or possibly an international jewel thief. Miss Olga told the audience about her dance school in Austin, and how successful their program was. Then she introduced her dancers—a girl named Anita Fleming, and James Jenkins—and she explained

ANDREW SMITH

how James and Anita had won second place last summer in the Junior National Championships for what she called their Pas de Deux, a ballet duet with a boy-and-girl team.

I was in awe of how brave James Jenkins must have been. The people of Blue Creek (thanks mostly to his dad) had determined that James Jenkins would be a standout quarterback, but he was the second-best fourteen-year-old boy in the entire nation at Pas de Deux, whatever that was.

When Miss Olga introduced them, James and Anita stepped out onto the stage from opposite sides. The crowd went as quiet as a thousand farmers witnessing the landing of an alien spacecraft in the middle of their onion fields. Anita was a black girl, tall and slender, stepping gracefully out and pinning herself motionless in the rear corner of the stage. Her hair was pulled back in a compact twist, and she wore white tights under an airy lavender dress that you could see through. I thought she easily could have been the prettiest girl I'd ever seen in my life. James Jenkins wore pale gray tights with white shoes and a tight-fitting white T-shirt tucked down into the top of his tights. And they both had expressions on their faces that looked so calm and confident, happy even. This was a James Jenkins—in real life—that nobody here had ever laid eyes on.

James looked directly at me (without moving his chin). I think he smiled a little bit, but it wasn't like a murderer's smile. His mouth moved upward maybe one-fifteenth of an inch, like a *danseur* would do, so that nobody could really tell if he smiled or not.

Then I did the thing that I had come here to do.

And I have to explain that what I did was definitely *not* something I would normally have ever done—not for anybody or anything. But I couldn't get over the fact that James Jenkins had kind of saved my life, and more than once, too. And I also couldn't get over how wrong I'd been about him all these years, but maybe that's exactly what living in a place like Blue Creek can do to people.

What I did was this: I reached down, grabbed the bottom of my T-shirt, and quickly pulled it off over the top of my head, so I was standing there at the front of the crowd, right next to the stage, bare chested in front of all these people attending Blue Creek Days.

I raised my fists in the air like I was crossing some kind of finish line, just to make certain James Jenkins (and the beautiful Anita Fleming) would really look at me.

REALIZATION NUMBER 2: Painting slogans on your own chest and belly while looking into a restroom mirror at a miniature golf course is very difficult.

Before I'd left Lily Putt's Indoor-Outdoor Miniature Golf Course, I had taken a bottle of the paint we used to touch up Rusty, our orange tinfoil-hat-wearing fiberglass T. rex, and painted this:

ANDREW SMITH

My *S* fell victim to the reversing powers of a restroom mirror.

James Jenkins saw it. His eyes darkened a little and turned down, and I noticed he gulped a quick breath, like he was startled. His cheeks turned a little red. Nobody in Blue Creek had ever seen ballet, and nobody had *ever* seen James Jenkins blush. And although the crowd was as quiet as they'd be if we were all stalking the same buck on a deer hunt, with my arms still raised I shouted this: "You're my hero, James Jenkins!"

I would bet it was the first time in history a bare-chested, kilt-wearing eleven-year-old Texan had painted his belly and yelled at a ballet performance.

A few people behind me clapped, but it sounded like an unsure round of applause.

I turned around and saw James's mother in the crowd. His dad wasn't there, though. Of course he wasn't. I was sure Kenny Jenkins was at the judging for the Macaroni and Cheese Cook-Off Challenge, which he would certainly win now.

I didn't care.

The music came on, and James and Anita began their Pas de Deux.

REALIZATION NUMBER 3: I may not understand anything at all about ballet, but I could still tell that James Jenkins was a—excuse me—heck of a talented *danseur*.

James could fly. He landed soundlessly, and when he lifted Anita Fleming, she transformed into a weightless floating spirit, and then their bodies would fold and collapse and soften and blend together like they were a single, incredible living creature.

When the music stopped, there was a hush in the audience like we had all collectively been punched in the gut. I looked back at James's mother. She was crying and had her hands folded in front of her mouth. I was kind of crying too, but I must have looked like an (excuse me) idiot, standing there shirtless in a kilt with "Go James" (with a backward *S*) painted on my belly in non-washable orange paint that would probably never come off. I turned back toward the stage, and the audience snapped out of their stunned silence and broke into applause.

James and Anita stood and faced the audience and bowed. In James's case, that meant lowering his chin about half an inch. Neither of the dancers showed any emotion. Their faces were perfect and calm, like this is what they were always meant to be doing—like the audience had been lucky enough to eavesdrop on something of such personal and perfect natural beauty that there was no space for words or thought. Then, noiselessly, James and Anita left the stage, and it was all over.

It really was all over.

I pulled my shirt on and ducked back through the crowd. It felt good. I didn't care about anything else. I was happy for my friend.

THERE'S NO SCORE

We start with a song recorded decades earlier, stuck in my head, trapped in a slow bend of time.

I had done what I wanted to do. Well, for the most part I did, that is.

And it was a strange thing, because I was happy and sad all at the same time. I especially did not want to talk to anybody after watching James Jenkins do what was so important to him. I headed out through the midway of the fair, determined to get back to Lily Putt's so I could lose myself behind the counter of the snack bar. It would be busy there, and I had added a special hamburger made with venison, sweet potatoes, and charred bitter greens to the menu. I thought maybe I'd send one over in a to-go package for Kenny Jenkins, to congratulate him on winning the Macaroni and Cheese Cook-Off Challenge while he was busy ignoring his son, just so maybe he could write about how horrible my food is in next week's Cook's Riot! column.

Nice work, Kenny Jenkins.

"Hey, Sam! Sam!"

I stopped walking.

James Jenkins was moving through the crowd behind me. His head and shoulders rose above the sea of people between us. He looked transformed. He looked like he'd just conquered the world. It was almost like he had grown a foot taller; or maybe I'd shrunk. He'd pulled on some track pants and was barefoot. I guess walking around a small-town fair in Texas when you're a boy dressed in very tight tights and ballet shoes makes you look as out of place as if you were wearing a kilt.

I guess James Jenkins and I were as outcast as outcasts could be.

And he still walked so slow, without moving his chin. James Jenkins was something else. How was it that a guy who could jump as high and far as James Jenkins, who could spin around faster than the drum of a washing machine, moved so painfully slowly?

Nice work, James Jenkins.

Before he caught up to me, I heard two more people say something about the Little Boy in the Well. One of them was wearing a PRAY FOR SAM T-shirt.

Then James said, "Hey."

And I said, "Hey."

It was awkward. We were never *not* awkward. Just like I was never *not* the Little Boy in the Well. At least James Jenkins was something else now, something new.

ANDREW SMITH

So I said, "You were incredible, James. And that Anita. Wow."

James Jenkins nodded, which is to say his chin moved up and down about one-tenth of an inch. He said, "She's the best."

"She's really pretty."

James said, "I know." And, "Why are you wearing that?"

Sometimes it was almost like I could completely forget I wore kilts. I looked down at my bare white twig-legs poking out from the hem of the red Clan Abernathy tartan. I said, "I ran out of pants."

James made his *huh* sound, a kind of whispered, tentative laugh. He needed to work on that.

"Well, I . . . uh . . . wanted to tell you thank you, Sam, for what you did. You know, getting Miss Olga to come out, and making me dance. And painting your chest and all," James said.

"Sorry. I know you hate it when people paint their bellies."

"Only for football," James said.

"Yeah. And Gatorade. You told me that."

It was so awkward, and all I wanted to do was get the (excuse me) heck away from Blue Creek Days.

James Jenkins didn't move his chin. He didn't move his eyes, either, but he was looking straight at me, or maybe he was looking at the top of my head—I couldn't tell. But he said, "I feel like you kind of saved my life."

Excuse me, but dang it, that made me choke a little.

I said, "Then we're even."

James Jenkins shook his head. It wasn't a major headshake, but it was significant movement for James Jenkins. He said, "There's no score."

"Okay."

"Well, I got to get back to my mom."

"I saw her. You made her cry," I said.

James Jenkins rolled his eyes, which meant they rotated upward about three degrees. He said, "She always cries when I dance."

"If you bring your mom over to Lily Putt's, I'll make you both some burgers, to say congratulations and stuff. And you can play golf. On the house," I said.

James said, "Thanks."

"No worries."

"You want to come over and hang out later?" James asked.

I nodded. It was a Texan-in-a-kilt nod, so anyone could see it. I said, "Sure."

James Jenkins turned to leave, but I stopped him. I said, "Hey. So what *was* your favorite part in *Dune*?"

James stopped. He turned around very slowly, without moving his chin. He said, "When Paul cried for Jamis."

"That part wrecked me too."

James Jenkins made his little *huh* sound and then turned to walk back to where his mother was waiting. I watched him as he cut through the crowd. People stopped him and shook his hand and slapped his shoulder, which is probably not what you're supposed to do to a ballet *danseur*. And even from where I was standing, I could see James Jenkins blush and smile—well, sort of smile.

And then it was almost like I had been trapped inside Blue Creek Days. On my way out of the fair, Karim stopped me as I passed the Science Club booth, shouting at me, "Sam! It worked! It really worked! We got something weird!"

I had forgotten all about the Science Club project. It probably had a lot to do with the fact that I didn't care about Science Club. I decided right then I was going to quit the club on Monday.

Hayley Garcia was making fine adjustments on our tuner. Bahar was rotating the small dish antenna, trying to capture the strongest signal, and Karim was waving his arms at me like a drowning victim caught in a riptide.

"Come here! Listen to this!" Karim shouted.

When I got to our table, I heard a crackling sputter like one of those preserved recordings of an early-times radio program, and a man's voice—twangy, Texan, and high-pitched.

Bahar said, "It keeps playing the same thing, over and over and over."

Hayley Garcia added, "We've heard it twelve—no, thirteen—times in a row now."

Hayley Garcia had penciled tally marks on an index card.

I leaned my head in closer to the speaker. It really was a radio program, but it was from way in the past. The man's voice said, "Happy New Year's Eve 1972, Fort Worth! We're wishing every one of you the merriest of celebrations, right here from the Stockyards, playing one of our all-time-favorite gospel songs tonight on the Bartleby Until Midnight show!"

I knew that voice.

And, of course, I knew the song, too. It was "I Will Walk with Him in the Garden of Blood," by Lily Abernathy, my great-grandmother.

I shook my head. I made James Jenkins's little *huh* sound through my nose and said, "That's really weird."

Karim nodded and affirmed, "*Really!*"

WITH YOUR LUCK, SAM?

It starts with conflicting signals.

"This is kind of a catchy tune," Karim said.

I'd heard "I Will Walk with Him in the Garden of Blood" so many countless times in my life that its catchiness had evolved into something more like water torture.

"We should look up the records to find out if this Bartleby Until Midnight show ever actually did broadcast from Fort Worth in 1972," Hayley Garcia, ever the scientist, ever the taskmaster of the Science Club, suggested.

"I'm sure I've heard Bartleby before," I said.

And as Hayley Garcia added another tally mark to her index card, and Bartleby welcomed in 1972 again, another sound, louder, blared over the loudspeakers that hung from utility poles along the midway.

It said this: "If anyone sees little Sam Abernathy in the fairgrounds, could you please send him over to the judging tent immediately? Sam Abernathy, please report to the judging tent."

(Excuse me.)

I would never *not* be "little" to pretty much everyone in Blue Creek, forever.

But I did not want to go to the judging tent. Why would I? So I could watch Kenny Jenkins win what he came here to win? I wanted to leave Blue Creek Days. I wanted to leave Blue Creek entirely. I realized I'd rather head out on a survival weekend with Dad and eat garbage than go to the judging tent.

"It's your mac and cheese!" Bahar said.

I shook my head. "It can't be. I didn't finish it in time this morning. I never got it into the oven."

Karim came around the side of our table. He grabbed my shoulder and said, "Maybe you're in trouble, then. Did you and James Jenkins get caught talking again where you're not allowed to? Come on, I'll go with you."

Karim walked with me over to the main tent, which had been pitched in the big dirt spillover lot behind the community center.

"You can't really get in trouble at Blue Creek Days, can you?" I asked.

I had gotten in trouble with James Jenkins so many times, I was beginning to develop a guilty conscience. And then I thought, maybe there are strict rules against painting your chest at a ballet demonstration.

And Karim, answering a question with a question, said, "With your luck, Sam?"

We went inside.

The place was dark and crowded. At the back of the tent was a long banquet table covered in white linen. There must have been twenty dishes set out—and all the food looked pretty much the same: yellow and blobby. What would you expect from a mac and cheese contest, anyway?

Mom, Dad, Evie, and Dylan were standing next to the table. They were talking to someone I recognized from all the times I'd sneak in and watch cooking programs on TV after bedtime—it was the celebrity chef Resa O'Hare, and she looked even more beautiful in real life than she did on television. I thought I'd faint when she looked at me and smiled.

Resa O'Hare, who clearly realized that Dad and I were probably the only people in the state of Texas wearing matching kilts, and miraculously made the connection, said, "This must be Sam!"

Then everybody started clapping, which was exactly the opposite of what I was expecting, since I had pretty much convinced myself that I was in trouble for painting my chest and taking off my shirt at a ballet demonstration.

Somehow, the dish of macaroni and cheese I had made (to be honest, it was orecchiete with Gorgonzola, pears, and prosciutto) had shown up here at the contest. Somehow, my dish had won first prize. I didn't understand how any of this could have been possible.

I half expected to find a talking armadillo and dancing

otters there with us inside the tent, but there were only people—and an awful lot of them too.

I was confused, and I was speechless.

Karim put an arm around my shoulders and shook me. "You did it, Sam! You won! I knew you could do it!"

I heard someone in the crowd say, "The Little Boy in the Well is a mighty fine chef!"

And someone else said, "Why's he dressed like that?"

(Excuse me.)

TAKING THE NEXT STEP

This story ends with a report on the bank robber Ethan Pixler that I did for my Social Studies class. I even wrote a skit, and James Jenkins was allowed to come in and play the part of Ethan Pixler. James wanted to make it a musical, but I can't dance.

It ends with my dad, who found the dish I'd prepared (but failed to put in the oven when I ran out of time), which he baked and brought to Blue Creek Days for me.

And it ends with Karim breaking up with Hayley Garcia because he quit the Science Club on the same day I did.

Karim already has a new girlfriend.

It ends with Kenny Jenkins, James Jenkins's dad and owner of Colonel Jenkins's Diner, who placed fourth out of twenty-two in the Great Blue Creek Days Macaroni and Cheese Cook-Off Challenge. I added the word *Great*, by the way. It was pretty great, after all, but not for Kenny Jenkins, who everyone had assumed was destined to win.

And the story ends with me and my dad, talking to each other and *listening* to each other about things.

It was an enormous truth for Dad.

But in the end he'd admitted that if he did exactly with his life what his father had wanted him to do, he would have probably been planting onion seeds in October as opposed to doing what he loved best, which was wearing his kilt, running Lily Putt's Indoor-Outdoor Miniature Golf Course, and helping his boy get a dish of orecchiete with Gorgonzola, pears, and prosciutto into the oven on time for the big contest.

It was a big step for my father.

Dad cried. I'd never seen my father cry. He told me he was sorry, and how it was a tough thing for him to recognize that his son could have ideas of his own—imagine that! Then he told me he loved me and was so proud of me, and I cried too and told Dad that I loved him. We were a bunch of crying messes, in our kilts, survival camping on a cold end-of-October weekend in the Tingle-Heacock State Wilderness Area. It was great. We didn't get any food or water that weekend, but it was the best time I'd ever had with Dad.

I would not have to go to Blue Creek Magnet School or get into AP Physics or invent whatever it was that Dad thought I needed to invent after graduating from MIT. Resa O'Hare was so astonished by what a little eleven-year-old eighth grader had done that she invited me to come to the high school where she taught—a private boarding school in Oregon with the nation's best Culinary Arts program for teens (even if I was only going to be twelve), where nobody would know anything about PRAY

FOR SAM or the Little Boy in the Well. It was scary for me to think about leaving Blue Creek by myself, but it was scarier for me to think about staying with all these Blue Creekers who had already filled in every blank they could think of about me.

The paint on my chest didn't come off for a week.

And this story ends with James Jenkins leaving Blue Creek too. A month after he danced for everyone at Blue Creek Days, after he performed in my skit about Ethan Pixler, James Jenkins moved to Austin with his mother and enrolled in high school there, which is where he belonged.

After all, James Jenkins is one of the smartest kids I know, and he's a real good example of what it means to be a human being too, in my opinion.

And this story ends with me, not looking down before I take the next step, not ever again.

ACKNOWLEDGMENTS

On a bright spring morning a few years ago as I was getting ready to leave New York City on a book tour that went back and forth across the country (and up into Canada as well), I had breakfast at a Momofuku place with Elizabeth Kossnar and my editor, David Gale. Can I drop names? Okay, we ran into Alessandra Balzer there, and she was very nice.

It was at this breakfast that David talked about the possibility of me writing a middle-grade novel, and we talked about doing one just about Sam Abernathy, a character I love very much. But who doesn't love Sam, right? So I started it, and I stopped; started it again, got pretty far, then stopped. Who knew that writing middle-grade is much more than merely a matter of writing YA with younger kids and no (excuse me) swears?

It took a while. And then I was back in New York, and David asked me again why I hadn't done my book about Sam yet. I told him I had but I was going through a weird time where I didn't really want anything of mine to be out in the daylight. It was like I'd been at the bottom of a well and had gotten quite comfortable there.

I guess David got me out of my well, and I had cultivated quite a cozy, affectionate Stockholm Syndrome–like connection to my well. And now here we are, up in the light. Thank you, David.

I've dedicated this book to Kelly Milner Halls, a wonderful person I've known since I was about fourteen years old. And I really do mean this: that if it is true that Andrew Smith writes friendships pretty well, it's because of the people in my life like Kelly. Much love and appreciation to you, Kelly.

And to my other friends who stick by me whether I'm in a well or not—I owe you everything: A. S. King, Z Brewer (and we must return to that place in Denver—you know, the place with the pie), Greg Neri, Gae Polisner, Michael Bourret, Carrie, E, my brothers with whom I share no DNA Matt and Jon, Jenny Paulsen, Michael Grant, and why am I afraid I'm leaving someone out?

I might be bad at making lists, but like Sam Abernathy, I'm a pretty good cook.

And all my friends—Ethan Pixler included—are invited down into my well for dinner.

ACKNOWLEDGMENTS

A READING GROUP GUIDE TO

The Size of the Truth

By Andrew Smith

About the Book

After falling into an abandoned well, four-year-old Sam Abernathy copes with his situation the only way he knows how: he befriends a delightfully sarcastic resident armadillo prankster named Bartleby. Bartleby inhabits the tunnels surrounding the hopelessly cramped well, and encourages Sam to explore the mazes and their secret treasures. The narrative then shifts to eleven-year-old Sam's eighth-grade year in a Texas small-town middle school where he's skipped two grades, resulting in an equally awkward sense of entrapment. Making hopeful attempts to express his true self and, once again, in need of escape from a life he feels helpless to influence, Sam finds a way to explore the deeply rooted fears, assumptions, and limitations that have led to his current situation. Traveling back and forth between Sam's experiences as a four-year-old in a well and an adolescent grades ahead of his peers, the book follows Sam's realization that some truths are more difficult to reach than others. It's only when Sam reaches out to James Jenkins in a selfless act of kindness that both boys begin to understand the need for reclaiming who they really are.

Discussion Questions

1. In what ways do you think the author captures a distinct middle school voice and tone? How credible did you find Sam as a narrator? Could you trust what was true for him? Explain your answers.

2. Would you consider this story to be plot-based, issue-driven, or character-driven, or a combination of each? Explain your answers.

3. What do you think of the book's cover design? What did it immediately suggest to you? Did it make you want to read the book?

4. Which character did you relate to most? What about that character did you identify or connect with? Which character was most unlike you? Explain your answer. Was there someone you admired most? If so, who, and for what reasons?

5. Consider the title, *The Size of the Truth*. What does it mean to you? Within the context of this story, how do you think Andrew Smith defines "truth"? Do you think different people can experience different truths?

6. How does the culture of Blue Creek, Texas, contribute to the unfolding of the story? How might the story have been different if it had been set in a bigger city?

7. Why might the author have chosen to tell the story by shifting between past and present? How did this affect the way you experienced the story? Does meeting Sam at two different ages make you feel like you understand him better?

8. Sam says, "I think middle school is the time in life when you first start to develop the grown-up habit of pretending everything's fine when it really is not." Do you agree with Sam? Why do you think he feels this way? He then says, "I began to feel as though I'd been transported to a strange planet where nothing was right." Have you ever felt this way? What, if anything, would you change about this "strange planet"? Do you have any advice to offer Sam? Is there anyone in your life you feel comfortable asking for advice about navigating middle school? Explain your answer.

9. Sam's parents thought they knew what was best for him with "their obsession about making sure I'd never have the freedom to fall into unseen holes in my future." Because of their efforts, Sam feels that "Nobody knew what would have been Sam, if choices had been left up to me." Do you think many eleven-year-olds feel the same way? Discuss with your peers. Is it difficult to be honest with your parents? Are there ever times you think you should question their judgment? Explain your answers.

10. We learn much about four-year-old Sam's character from his experiences with Bartleby in the well, such as his strong desire to please and avoid disappointing his parents, his emotional resiliency, and his heightened curiosity and imagination. What else do we learn about Sam while he is in the well? What traits does he continue to demonstrate into eighth grade? How does he express these traits in his adolescent experiences? How do you think his experience in the well shaped his childhood?

11. When Bartleby entered the story, what did you make of him as a character? What is his role in Sam's story? How does he affect Sam? When Sam disconnected from his present reality for periods of time, did you think he was dreaming? Or was he suffering from hallucinations or delusions? Cite references from the text to support your conclusions.

12. One of the novel's major themes is feeling trapped. Sam experiences several forms of physical and emotional entrapment, including inside a well, a nightmare, a tunnel, a school, a town, and a family that, although well-intentioned, doesn't understand who he really is. Have you ever felt trapped? If so, how did you handle it? Explain your answer. In what ways is Sam's perceived tormentor, James Jenkins, also trapped? What are some of the other themes or main ideas that the author conveys to readers?

13. Bartleby's scenes are rich in imagery. For example, consider the maze of tunnels, a secret treasure room, talking animals, and Ethan

Pixler's coffin buried fifty-four feet underground. How do these images help you understand Sam's situation? What other images stand out to you? How do they relate to the rest of the story?

14. Why do you think Sam followed Bartleby through the tunnels instead of waiting for rescue? What would you have done if you were Sam?

15. Which passages or scenes did you find to be the most humorous or intriguing? How about the most insightful, disturbing, or unique? Which did you find most thought-provoking or surprising?

16. While in the well, Sam is often more confused than he is frightened, and he has conflicting ideas of what Bartleby's all about. For example, Bartleby tells Sam to "Quit being a quitter . . . I'll tell you when we go back. But you have to trust me." Bartleby then says, "I'm lying again!" and "You really shouldn't be so trusting of strangers, Sam!" What is Bartleby teaching Sam about trust? What is the author saying about trust?

17. Beneath the humor, Bartleby teaches Sam some important things about growing up. What are some of the more profound or important messages Bartleby conveys to Sam? Do you think Sam understands some of what Bartleby was trying to convey now that he's eleven? What are some of the things you didn't understand at four, but understand now?

18. Sam reflects, "Maybe deep down I still blamed James Jenkins for throwing the ball so high, and for falling into that well when I was four years old." Sam also holds James responsible for his "extreme claustrophobia and not talking for two years . . ." How do Sam's assumptions about James and his feelings of being James's victim initially play into Sam's adolescence? How did it affect their relationship throughout elementary school and into middle school? What does Sam eventually understand about James as their friendship deepens?

19. At what point in the story did you begin to form your own opinion of James Jenkins, regardless of what Sam believed to be the truth? Cite specific passages or clues. Why can it be difficult to change your opinion of someone? Why do you think Sam continued to believe this narrative about James for so long?

20. James was described as a boy "who nobody liked and everyone was afraid of." What do you think motivated him to act the way he did? What more would you like to know about James? What perspective does he bring to the story?

21. Sam's father insists that Sam experience basic survival skills while camping, but these skills only account for a small part of what Sam needs to survive eighth grade. What other skills does Sam need? Discuss with your peers. Why do you think Sam was unhappy about making the jump from sixth to eighth grade? Think about differences between his mental and emotional intelligence.

22. Describe Sam's dad and what he values. What does it take for Sam to be able to communicate truthfully with his father about what he really wants? Discuss how their relationship changes throughout the story.

23. What role do adults play in this story? Consider Coach Bovard, the homeroom teacher Mr. Mannweiler, Kenny Jenkins, Mrs. Jenkins, and Mr. and Mrs. Abernathy. Cite at least one passage that defines each of these secondary characters. What influence do they have on Sam and James? Is there evidence that they tried to help either boy and their relationship? Do you think they were aware of any issues between the two boys?

24. What issues, if any, remain unresolved or uncertain at the end of the book? For example, how do you account for the Bartleby Until Midnight radio show captured by the Science Club experiment during Blue Creek Days? Explain your reasoning.

25. Did you find the ending satisfying? Explain your answer. What do you think life will be like for Sam and James after they leave Blue Creek next year? Discuss with your peers.

26. Has anything you've read about in this story changed your thoughts or opinions about the world around you? What have you learned about other people? What have you learned about yourself? Do you think you might do things differently in the future as a result of reading this book? Explain your answers.

Extension Activities

1. While visiting Ethan Pixler's underground treasure room, four-year-old Sam mentions, "I knew a few things about bats, living in the region of Texas where Blue Creek was . . ." Bat Conservation International (BCI) protects the largest urban bat colony in North America, found under the famous Congress Avenue "bat" Bridge in downtown Austin, Texas, which it promotes as an ecotourism destination. The Statesman Bat Observation Center next to the bridge provides a viewing area for tourists to witness nightly bat flights. BCI also works globally to protect bats and their habitats.

Research BCI's operation. Examine the unique culture of one of the world's most endangered animals, the often misrepresented yet sophisticated and gentle animals populating the area in which Andrew Smith has set this story.

2. The experience of trauma affects sensations and perceptions, emotional understandings, and responses. Having lived through a traumatic event, Sam, until his eleventh year, could not recall anything that took place during his time in the well. He was unable to speak for two years after the event, and subsequently adopted imagined perceptions and assumptions of reality. Research the symptoms of post-traumatic stress disorder, citing examples from the text that either support or negate the idea that Sam was suffering from PTSD. Then research the treatments for PTSD, and how people can support friends and family going through it. How might Sam's family have been able to better support him?

3. Sam suffers from extreme claustrophobia as a result of his trauma, characterized by an irrational fear of being trapped inside small spaces. Research the possible causes, symptoms, and treatment of claustrophobia. What advice would you have for Sam after doing this research? Pretend you are Sam's friend, and write him a letter of support.

4. Does Sam's passion for cooking and James's passion for dance inspire you to follow your own passion? Research your most desired field of interest. What would you have to do to prepare for a future in that field? Where and when would you have to study, train, or practice in order to proceed with your chosen career or interest? What barriers or challenges might you have to overcome? What sacrifices might you have to make? Are you willing to do these things to accomplish your dream?

5. Asking the question "What is truth?" leads to many answers, and possibly even more questions. Many say it's a question that cannot be answered. In *The Size of the Truth,* each character has his or her own truth as they know it. But can there be conflicting truths? Andrew Smith asks readers to consider the personal truths or beliefs that his characters initially hold, as well as the eventual truths they come to realize as they ask important questions of themselves and each other.

What ideas has Sam held to be true, only to realize his assumptions have distorted his reality? Discuss these ideas and implications with your peers. Then choose one or two other characters, and examine the truths and assumptions they've made that have defined their life experiences. How are their experiences similar or different to Sam's?

Then consider your own personal truths. Can you make a list of statements you believe to be true? Are they necessarily the only truths? Might there be other perceptions or opinions that could change those beliefs? Pair up with a few classmates to discuss, and share your findings with the class.

6. Read two earlier novels by Andrew Smith. In *Winger* and *Stand-Off*, readers fell in love with Ryan Dean West, a high school student at the Pine Mountain Academy private boarding school in Oregon. It was there, in *Stand-Off*, that Smith first introduced us to freshman Sam Abernathy, Ryan Dean's roommate. You'll find that life is anything but predictable for Sam once he leaves Blue Creek, Texas.

This guide was written in 2018 by Judith Clifton, M.Ed, MS, Educational and Youth Literary Consultant, Chatham, MA.

This guide has been provided by Simon & Schuster for classroom, library, and reading group use. It may be reproduced in its entirety or excerpted for these purposes.

Turn the page for a sneak peek at
Bye-Bye, Blue Creek,
the sequel to *The Size of the Truth.*

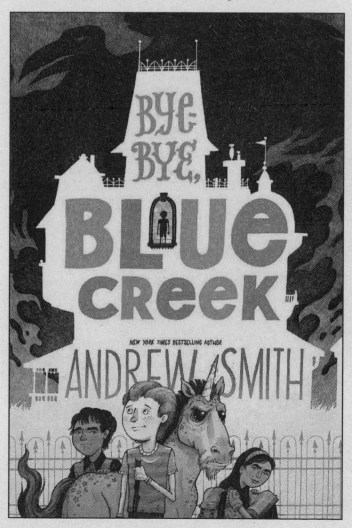

ON SAYING GOODBYE

No one likes goodbyes.

Goodbyes are like bad haircuts: it takes time to get over the shock and adjust to the "new you," and it's never a pleasant process.

The short summer before I went away to Pine Mountain[1] seemed to be a long, drawn-out, and awkward goodbye. I had already said goodbye to my friend James Jenkins, who had moved away to Austin during the school year, and now there were all these other things to say goodbye to, lining up like a gauntlet of extended family on a chilly Thanksgiving evening when you're the first one out the door: My friends Karim and Bahar, Blue Creek[2], Lily Putt's Indoor-Outdoor Miniature Golf Course[3], Mom and Dad, Dylan and Evie, that awful Colonel Jenkins' Diner, and everything about Texas that had grown to be a part of me—right down to the color of the dirt and the

---

1 Pine Mountain is a private boarding school in Oregon. I won a scholarship to go there, which was something I wanted more than anything else in the world—up until a few weeks before I had to leave, that is.

2 The town where I grew up, which is in Texas, which is also far away from Oregon.

3 My family's business.

smell of the air in April. I had to say goodbye to all of it.

And although going to school at Pine Mountain was the one thing I wanted more than anything else in the world, I also didn't want to leave everything else behind.

It was a real predicament, and I kept telling myself how grown-up all this made me feel, but if this is what being a grown-up was like, you could keep it. Because I didn't know what to do.

I didn't want to say goodbye, but I had already gone too far to change my mind.

Besides, I didn't want people to think I was too anything—too small, too young, too *sensitive*—to do something as daring as leave for boarding school in Oregon (which I already knew was going to be colder, rainier, greener, and lonelier than Texas), even if I would have agreed with anyone who told me those things.

So there I was: stuck.

Stuck and wondering how to manage all those long goodbyes.

ICED TEA NUMBER SEVEN, OR HERE COME THE SPIDERS AGAIN

Anyone who's ever left home to live all alone for the first time in their life knows exactly what it feels like to have thousands of stampeding spiders in their stomach.

And when you're twelve years old, and small for your age on top of that, the spiders can feel like they're the size of rabbits.

What if I get scared in the middle of the night and there's no one to talk to?

What if I have an attack of claustrophobia[4]?

I didn't tell anyone in my family about how nervous I was. I didn't want them to try to talk me out of going away to boarding school. Because talking me out of it would have been easier than getting a dirty look from Kenny Jenkins at Colonel Jenkins's Diner for ordering a large iced tea *without* sugar in it. And that was very, very easy to do.

There were exactly seventeen days of summer left before

---

4 I have a very bad case of claustrophobia, on account of my having been trapped in an abandoned well when I was four years old.

my family (which consisted of Mom, Dad, my brother Dylan, and my sister Evie) was going to pack me up and make the drive all the way from Blue Creek, Texas, to Pine Mountain, Oregon, where I was going to enroll in high school (at twelve years old, no less) and move into a dormitory full of grown-up boys, and share a room with some stranger who would probably end up tormenting me the way a cat toys with a mouse before eventually murdering it.

Here come the rabbit-sized spiders again.

"I'm kind of anxious about starting ninth grade too, Sam," Bahar said.

"But you're fourteen years old. You've already done all the in-between grades," I told her.

In school, I skipped ahead two years—the in-between grades from sixth to eighth. To some people, it was like my life was moving faster. To me, it was like two years of unread pages had been torn from my biography.

Bahar was the cousin of my best friend, Karim. She was one of those rare older kids who was nice to me when she wasn't *forced* to be polite, and she would always stand up to the pressure that other fourteen-year-olds might put on her for being friends with a smallish boy who was only twelve.

I guess that made us friends, too, along with all the other things we had in common.

We had the same taste in tea, for one thing. Bahar liked iced tea with no sugar in it, and I did too, which is why Kenny

Jenkins had been giving us dirty looks, since he always had to make them up special just for us when we came in[5]. One time Kenny Jenkins said to us (in as disgusted a tone as I'd ever heard him use), "You'd think you kids were from California or something, the way you drink that tea the same way West Coast snobs would. Well I'm telling you right now: I don't serve *kale* here."

Clearly, Kenny Jenkins had no idea just how delicious sautéed kale with garlic, vegetable stock, and red wine vinegar really was.

Bahar and I always met at Colonel Jenkins's for iced tea and dirty looks on Saturday afternoons. Well, not always. This was the seventh time we did; the routine just kind of started one time during the last week of eighth grade when I was walking home from the miniature golf course my family owned. And like being nervous about going away to Pine Mountain, I also didn't tell my mom and dad (or Karim) about meeting up with Bahar on Saturdays. Because it didn't really matter, did it?

It wasn't like I had a crush on Bahar.

I'd never had a crush on anyone in my life.

---

5 Nobody in Blue Creek ever did something as non-Texan as ordering not-sweet tea at Colonel Jenkins's

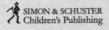